A NEST OF HOOKS

THE IOWA SCHOOL OF LETTERS AWARD FOR SHORT FICTION

A Nest of Hooks
by Lon Otto

UNIVERSITY OF IOWA PRESS Ψ IOWA CITY

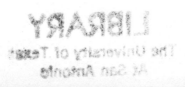

The previously published stories in this collection appear by permission:
"A Very Short Story," *Atlantic Review* (De-
cember 1976).
"With Horse People," *Great River Review* 1
(1977).
"Background Music" and "I'm Sorry That
   You're Dead," *Chance Music: Gallimaufry 10
   & 11* (1977).

Library of Congress Cataloging in Publication Data

Otto, Lon, 1948–
   A nest of hooks.

   (The Iowa School of Letters award for short fiction)
   I. Title. II. Series.
PZ4.O912Ne [PS3565.T79]   813'.5'4   78-16507
ISBN 0–87745–089–7
ISBN 0–87745–090–0 pbk.

University of Iowa Press, Iowa City 52242
© 1978 by The University of Iowa. All rights reserved
Printed in the United States of America

Prize money for the Award is provided by a
grant from the Iowa Arts Council.

TO MY MOTHER AND FATHER

CONTENTS

A NEST OF HOOKS

THERE WAS A PLUMP, PLAIN GIRL in my grade school class, and in the eighth grade she made up a story about the most popular boy and the most popular girl in the class. It was about them getting married and then driving off very very far on their honeymoon, and then going to bed together for the first time, about their bodies lying very very close to each other, about him being very very gentle with her.

The Story

She showed the story to me because I wrote stories, and this was her first story. I didn't know what to say about it, I just gave it back. I was embarrassed for her and just gave the piece of lined notebook paper back to her without saying anything. She was not a very good student; I imagine she read many romance magazines.

She passed the story around the class then. I watched them passing it from desk to desk. The girls who said anything said it was very beautiful, and the boys teased the most popular boy about it, who finally grabbed it from somebody and tore it up. The girl who wrote the story didn't seem to mind, and soon everybody forgot about it.

With Horse People

HE HAD NEVER RIDDEN A HORSE. He didn't want to, and he wasn't going to. He had a potentially bad back, and couldn't afford to cripple himself. He wasn't afraid of horses. Far from it. But neither was he going to make a fool of himself.

She was driving; three of her friends were in the back. They were horse people, as she was, and they were driving to a stable to see a horse she thought she wanted to buy. They had been up late the night before, and he wished he were back in bed, or sitting at the breakfast table, reading the Sunday paper, drinking coffee. But far from it. He was being driven into strange country, with horse people.

They were off the freeway now, driving on county roads through the dirty, cold drizzle. He was going to destroy his shoes in horse shit, and a big, potentially rabid collie was going to attack him, and the goddamned horse was going to break his leg, at best, because he walked behind it into its kicking range. "My God!" they would shout at him as he rolled in the muck, white with pain, "you *never* walk behind a chestnut hunter without first tapping him twice on the left shank to let him know it's all right!" They would turn to the snorting, evil-mouthed monster, then, and stroke it, and speak to it in soft, consoling voices. It would be a goddamned slug-eyed horse, he decided. They were the most vicious, he thought, the slug-eyed ones. He repeated the word to himself. Slug-eyed. It sounded right.

They turned off the asphalt road onto one of gravel, arrow-straight between fields plowed black, and then, at a sign that still said, but only barely, "Val-Lee Stables," they slithered onto a rutted, muddy lane. It was a wretched place. There was no house, only a few little cinder block sheds, sagging wire fences, a great deal of mud, and one low and one large barn of rusting corrugated steel. A few depraved sheep huddled in a pen with a wary, cynical pony, and bantam roosters stuck their heads out of wooden crates and crowed unpleasantly.

No one seemed to be around, although an old pickup truck was parked to one side of the lane. It might have been there for weeks. He suggested that they wait in the car until someone appeared, but they thought the owner was probably waiting for them in the barn.

They got out and plowed ahead of him toward the big door, badly hung from an overhead track. He saw them disappear behind it, more pulling it away from the barn side than sliding it back. He followed gingerly. They wore high boots, and he envied the carelessness with which they splashed through the horse-stirred slime of the stable yard. He edged forward, tacking along a few boards that lay about randomly, calculating the impossible leaps between them. He made it to the barn door finally, with almost half his shoe tops miraculously still dry. Stepping into the barn, his right foot sank to the ankle in ooze that was troughed treacherously under the door's track.

He stopped cursing after a while, and was futilely trying to dry his reeking foot on the sawdust that covered the barn floor when a very small girl trotted past haughtily on the littlest pony he had ever seen. A somewhat larger version of that girl followed on a fat, sluggish animal, half-horse, half-pony. They both rode without saddles, and the larger girl lashed at her mount with a long crop, forcing it from time to time to break into a shambling gallop for a few steps.

His eyes adjusted to the brown gloom; she was standing with her friends by another door at the far end of the barn. She seemed to have forgotten him, as he knew she would. Inside, at least, it was relatively dry; he watched his step carefully. They were waiting for a young woman to bring in the horse from some unimaginable mudhole of a pasture. He sat down on a bale of hay and watched the two little girls urge their horses at a wooden barricade — a gray fence rail set about ten inches off the ground on old rubber traffic cones laid sideways. The tiny pony danced smartly to the side for all its rider's screaming demands, and the fat half-horse, half-pony stepped over the obstacle carefully, knocking the rail down with a little flip of its last hoof. If he had been that animal he would have rolled over on the kicking, screaming little monster, and then he would have walked away as if nothing had happened.

The young woman was leading in a dark-brown horse, its coat matted with dirt and rain. As they gathered around it, he crossed the barn to see what was going on. He had read a lot of stories about horse trading, and this interested him. The owner was not there yet, so the young woman left them to examine the horse by themselves.

The four horse people moved about the patient animal confidently, efficiently, pointing out invisible irregularities and an occasional strong point. It was "down," that was the immediate judgment (apparently unfavorable). It had been fat once (apparently good), judging from the loose skin on its ass. "A little thin in the haunches," one would say, "good hocks." "The frogs are in bad shape, but they'll come around." "Isn't his neck too short to be a jumper?" "Check the slope of his croup."

He watched them from a little distance. "How about them slug-eyes?" he muttered, but no one heard him. He laughed very hard when she tried to lift a right front hoof while one of her friends was still holding up the left rear, nearly toppling the horse. He moved in and patted it on its vast side, casually. The coarse, close hair felt less like that of an animal than the fabric of some massive piece of furniture. He tried to edge in close when she drew back the grotesque, mobile lips to look in the horse's proverbial mouth, but all he could see was a mass of tangled yellow ivory, wet and menacing.

No one seemed eager to ride the horse, which surprised him. Instead they led it about by turns, the others observing a supposed stiffness in one leg, and an irregular, canted movement even he could see. Clearly no one thought the horse was worth buying, yet they kept this up for a long time, finally unhaltering and releasing it into the rain-dank pasture behind the barn. One of her friends ran trottingly at the jumping barricade and leaped it with a whoop, demonstrating to the little girls' horses how it was done, driving himself on with encouraging shouts and loud slaps on his thighs.

She took his arm as they left the barn. It was cold as hell in the fine drizzle, and she asked him if he had been too bored. It was interesting, he assured her. He gave up his shoes for lost. He helped her load her unused saddle and bridle back into the trunk and half listened to the running discussion of stables and shows and breeds and farriers and tack as they drove the long way back to the city.

They dropped off her friends and then went to a hamburger restaurant for something to eat. After ordering she reached over and gave his arm a fierce squeeze. "No more horse talk, babe," she said, "I promise." He patted her hand. "It's all right," he said. "It was educational." After a moment he asked, casually, "You were never really interested in that slug-eyed nag, were you?" She looked at him, puzzled: "Slug-eyed? What's that?" "Oh come on," he laughed, "you know." "Slug-eyed?" she asked again. "Sure," he said, "slug-eyed. Just about the most slug-eyed horse I ever saw." She nodded slowly. "Slug-eyed."

Her Hair

HE WAITED FOR HER OUTSIDE the theater, and when she came toward him it was with the pleased, defiant, defensive look of someone who has just had a haircut or a hairdo or is wearing new clothes. She had had a hairdo, a permanent which made her normally straight hair bushy and three-dimensional. "How do you like it?" she demanded as they went in and bought their tickets for the movie and bought popcorn and soda and found their seats.

"Well," he said. He leaned away for perspective, reached out and touched it tentatively here and there. "It looks good on you," he said finally. "Yes, I like it."

"No you don't," she said. "You liked it better the old way. Everybody does." It didn't seem to bother her very much. Screw 'em, her voice said. He thought hard. He couldn't really remember how it had been before. He had only known her for a little while, and, like a picture of someone you have not seen in a long time, her present appearance obscured all previous images. The day, the scattered stars. In fact, although he would never admit it, he had mostly noticed her breasts when they had been together before, that and her intense dark eyes.

"You used to wear it tied up in a scarf," he said.

"Only when it was dirty," she said. They watched the movie, which he liked, and she liked a lot. He didn't know her very well. He touched her altered hair from time to time with his finger tips. She looked like a rock star, he decided in the flickering darkness, one that screams a lot. She noticed him watching her and hissed at him sharply. She really thought the movie was important. She wanted him to watch the movie and leave her damn hair alone. He watched her furtively. Her hair gave her a certain look of wildness that was attractive, but also, at first, intimidating. They went to his place afterwards and talked for four hours.

They became very good friends. They got to know each other. He came to like her assertive, space-filling hair, and often felt himself in brushing, electric contact with it when she was not there. They were together a lot.

And then she said she was going to go away soon, in less than a month, and he understood that he was not going to be touching or even seeing her hair much more. And shortly after that, before she left, she had her hair done again. Her friend Lily did it for her again. She had done it the first time, too, Lily, one of the few radical feminist beauty operators in the Upper Midwest.

There was now a new intensity to her hair. Where before her hair had filled his space, the air he breathed, now her hair seized the air from out of his mouth, it held the light, as if angrily loving, in its tight curls. "I'm lost," he said as he tried to follow a path in her hair. Her hair held him like a labyrinth and sent him spinning out again and again. It was hard to think about her hair, especially the first few days, without an elaborate tightness behind his breastbone.

"You're being silly," she told him when he tried to explain all this. "It's just hair. It's just my hair, trying to look like I want it to look." Still, he watched her riding her horse shortly before she left, and he thought her hair interfered with the sunlight, somehow, and that when she made the horse jump, her hair made the arc sharper than it could have been, and horse and rider tangled bodies and minds and floated there an impossible moment before clipping again along the hard dust toward him.

Then she left, and she was gone a long time. In a picture of her, her hair was full of shadows, it flowed into the shadows that stood silently behind her. He studied her picture but learned nothing from it, and her hair told him nothing, being full of shadows. She was in the desert, thousands of miles from him, but her picture said nothing even of that.

When, after a long time, she came back, her hair burned against his lips, and he cried out in surprise. She was shy and fierce, in the old way, and tried to explain. "It must be the desert air that does that," she said.

"Have you been to see Lily?" he asked, wary and suspicious, but she laughed, "I haven't seen Lily yet. Don't worry. I think this is just a temporary thing." But even as she spoke the common objects in the room, the rocks, the table, melted, and shapes shifted, and he felt himself drawn down; fall blind into the timeless, unmapped, starry country of her hair.

THE WHITE ARAB GELDING plunged and jerked against the longe line at his nose; martingale and side-reins snapped his head back as he reared or tucked low, trying to buck. Again she snapped the long, light whip that never touched him, and again he bucked, backed away, pulling her across the soft earth and sawdust

Terror

footing of the indoor ring. She snapped the whip hard, hauled back on the longe line. "Trot!" she said, "trot, dammit!" He jumped back once more; reared. Then, suddenly obedient, he began trotting in the circle described by the twenty-foot rope. She moved in a little circle of her own in the center, following him, keeping herself focused on his driving hindquarters, the long whip trailing back from her other hand. "Canter!" she said, and after a moment's hesitation he shifted into the rolling gait that she wanted. "Good," she murmured, following him in her little controlling circle in the middle. "Good." When he slipped back into a trot she had only to raise the whip and speak to him once before he resumed cantering, circling mechanically in the cold, damp ring, his hooves ringing now and then on small stones, sometimes clashing together with a louder, hollow sound.

As the woman and horse moved in their small and large circles, the man leaned against the wooden railing, watching them, his back turned to the row of tie stalls that faced the ring. The stalls were almost all occupied, the horses having been brought in to be fed. They ate steadily, their tails to him. He stamped his feet on the cold concrete, buried his hands deeper in his coat.

When they were done here, then he could go home and take a hot bath and eat supper. When her horse was shod and she had finished her riding lesson and groomed her horse, fed him a last apple or carrot, then he could go out to his car and drive them through the late winter darkness on rutted, frozen roads and narrow county roads and the highway and the interstate back into the lighted city where he would forget the rank, steaming smell of the stable. He would drop her off at her apartment, she would not ask him up, though she might, perhaps, and he would drive through residential streets to his home, park in his garage and step finally into his warm kitchen, leaving his shoes in the entranceway.

A door in the wall across the ring slid open and a man in a T-shirt and heavy leather apron crossed the ring toward him. It was Dave, the farrier, who was to reset her horse's shoes before her evening lesson. "That's the way," the farrier shouted, climbing up on the railing beside him. "Run her legs off, burn up some of that orneriness." The woman hadn't had a chance to exercise the horse in several days, and it was stiff and jumpy from confinement in the ten-by-ten box stall. The farrier perched himself on the rail beside the man, who was grateful for the company, and followed the movement of the horse closely. "She's forging pretty bad, all right," the farrier observed after a moment. The man looked at him, and the farrier explained, "Her hooves are hitting together. Forging. We'll have to change the angle of her hooves a little, slow up them rear feet. Now, if she was running barefoot, Mother Nature would take care of it." The farrier's shaggy hair curled at his neck, dark with sweat in the cold stable.

In a few minutes the woman finished longeing the horse and led him back to the enclosed double line of stalls behind the far wall of the ring. She snapped slack chains to his halter from each side of the walkway and fed him an apple from the palm of her hand, saying comforting, encouraging words to him. "Oh, I love you so much!" she said to the horse, her arm hugging his neck. "You know I do," she said, "you know I do."

"She'll be all right," the farrier said, patting the horse's side and neck. "We'll get along fine, won't we," he said, scratching at the base of his forelock, wrapping his hand a moment around one startled ear, drawing the head down, then releasing it. "You have to let them know who's boss," he said. "That's the name of the game."

As the farrier straightened out the clinched-over nails in the first front hoof and pried off the shoe, the woman watched closely, squatting on her booted heels beside him. The man leaned back against the rough boards behind her, then squatted beside her, then rose and wandered around the other side of the horse. He examined the neatly arranged tools in the farrier's work box — pincers, small pry-bars, crooked-bladed hoof knife, sledgehammer, nails, brass caliper of some sort — and envied, as he always did, professionals working with tools, people who knew what they were doing. The woman, squatting beside the farrier, had the air of a colleague rather than a client.

The man stood, walked off toward the far end of the stable. In the closed area of the stalls the air was thick with the smell of manure and urine. He looked at his watch; it was after six. Her car was in the shop, so he had picked her up after work to bring her out for her lesson, which wouldn't begin until seven. He hadn't had anything to eat, and he hadn't had a chance to change his clothes. But when she had called the office to ask him to take her to the stable, it was the first time they had spoken in more than a week. He had decided that he didn't care, and then she had called.

He peered into a lightless stall, decided it was empty, then noticed a dark-brown horse standing motionless in back. If it had not been merely a convenience for her. If she had not merely needed a ride to the stable and thought of him, as one who knew the way by heart. If she. If she and he. But that was over; this sudden friendliness between them where there had been tension in good and bad times proved it was over. Which was why he had said, sure, yes, I'll pick you up after work. What was why? What did she want? He turned back, brushing something, straw or something, from his coat sleeve.

There had not been much progress. The farrier talked constantly and worked with an agonizing slowness. He clipped a ragged crescent from the front edge of a hoof and tossed it to the old, fat labrador that had been watching. As the dog grabbed the scrap and chewed at it, growling ecstatically, the farrier leaned against the horse and explained why dogs like hoof parings so much, and told them about a collie he had had when he was a kid, who was scared to death of horses but would come cowering and cringing around when someone was shoeing. The farrier was wiry and boyish, good-looking. As he told his stories he grinned frequently, baring his widely spaced front teeth. The man remembered something he had been told at a party the summer before, a cookout in the pasture of another stable. The woman had told him that most of the horse owners in this country are women, and farriers were said to get a lot of incidental sex. The man thought of Gerard Manley Hopkins' "Felix Randal."

There had been a farrier at that cookout, not Dave, a different one, a big, beefy man, silent and sullen, arrogant. The man had never met this farrier, had never met any farrier before. The man was a stranger to most of the horse people at the cookout, and had only known the woman for a few weeks. He sat on the tailgate of a pickup truck and watched the huge fire, drinking beer with the silent farrier. After a while the farrier loosened up a little and began picking up some of the younger women and pretended to be about to throw them into the fire. The women squealed and protested, and one tall, angry, rawboned woman, sitting on the ground before the fire, said, "When a woman says *no,* it doesn't *necessarily* mean, 'Overpower me!'" She was very sarcastic. Nobody except the man seemed to hear her, and she repeated the statement several times. The man sat on the tailgate, opening another beer, and wondered if he should tell the farrier to cut it out, but that would have been another male fantasy, and might well have ended in humiliation.

He wasn't sure what the woman would have wanted. On the way to the party, the woman had told him she didn't want to go to New York with him. After the cookout, walking arm in arm with him across the hilly pasture, she asked him what he thought of Ed. "The farrier?" he said. "I liked him at first.

He seemed what a farrier should be. Afterwards, he was just another asshole bully."

"You were expecting Felix Randal," she laughed. It was the truth. "Kay wants to sleep with him," the woman said. Kay was her best friend among the horse people. The man snorted in disbelief, and the woman said, "Well, he *is* awfully attractive." He couldn't figure her out. And later, when he had returned from New York and she talked about living together, he felt a sudden panic which must have shown on his face, for she had laughed out loud. Later, he changed his mind, but thought that she had changed, too, and so he said nothing, and they just slid along in a relationship that kept him constantly confused and uneasy, even when most happy.

Having finished talking about his dog, Dave hunkered down again beside the hoof he was working on, cleaned the frog with a blunt hook, checked the angle with the yellow brass gauge. He told them the angle in meaningless degrees. "Now, some farriers," he said, "would give her special built-up shoes to stop that forging." He held the hoof cocked on the heavy leather apron covering his thighs. "But me," he said, "I try to let Mother Nature take care of it. Just give her a little better angle," he said, working on the hoof with a big rasp, "then let Mother Nature do her thing." The farrier then told them about the old Indian in Montana who had taught him everything he knew about horses. He told them what he had learned in farrier school, and he told them what he learned from books. "Following Mother Nature," he said, "that's the name of the game."

When the farrier finally came to the fitting of the first shoe, it was nearly time for her lesson, though her instructor had not yet arrived. The farrier filled his mouth with the sharp shoeing nails; as he was about to tap home the first nail, he told them, through the nails, how important the first two nails were, and then he spat out all the nails and showed them how the nail was curved on one side, straight on the other side from point to head, so it would curve out through the hoof wall, rather than digging back into the quick. "You have to listen to Mother Nature," the farrier said. "She says she don't want nails in the quick. That's the name of the game. Kick your head in otherwise."

By the time the farrier had finished the two front hooves, it was a half hour past the time of the woman's lesson. Her instructor strode in then, a tall, thin woman with glasses, and insisted they begin at once. And so the woman saddled and bridled her horse and led him into the ring half-shod, while the farrier began work on another horse. "You take your time," the farrier shouted to her, as she disappeared through the passageway into the ring. "I'll finish her up when you're done. I aim to please, that's the name of the game."

The man watched the farrier begin the ear-scratching routine with the new horse and was going to stay there, but then he followed the woman into the open arena and crossed over to the other side. From behind the railing he watched her circle the ring under the glittering glassed eye and furious orders of the instructor. When the woman's hands were not straight enough, or her heels not low enough, or her back not erect enough, the instructor would shout at her savagely, as if personally insulted by each invisible error. And yet the woman's body seemed to him to move in perfect harmony with the horse: formal, controlled. Her jaw was set with concentration, and her lips were tight and pale. Her eyes looked straight ahead without emotion. From behind the far wall came the muffled sounds of the farrier's hammer pounding a shoe into shape.

The man's feet were growing painfully cold. He stamped on the concrete and thought about horses' hooves and iron shoes. The woman was taking the horse across low jumps now. The man was hungry and cold, but watched her for a while more, his throat tightening each time she approached the hurdle. Finally he gave in to his discomfort and retreated into the club room that was built into a corner of the stable. In the room there was a picture window that looked out into the arena; he stood before it, watching the woman and horse, silent through the glass, the instructor's harsh voice indistinct.

After a few minutes the man went to buy a soda from the machine that stood in one corner. The room was shabby and comfortable, warm, furnished with old stuffed chairs, a sofa, hideous lamps on blond end tables, and a television that was always on. The prettiest of several girls who worked at the stables was sitting on the sofa, watching television. The man picked up a horse magazine from the stack on one of the end tables, sat down with it, and watched the girl, who was really very pretty, watching the show. Like everyone there she wore boots, Levis, flannel shirt, and down vest. She looked good, lounging on the old couch, watching television without expression.

Another time when he had been out to the stable, this girl had come into the club room with a pail of dark water and a bottle of Lysol, her arm black to the elbow, stinking. "Been cleaning out my gelding," she had announced, and she and the woman had laughed, discussing what worked best for that unpleasant job. Another time he had watched the woman do it to her own horse, dipping her fingers in petroleum jelly, then reaching far up into the penis sheath of the edgy horse, dragging out a muddy, tar-like crud on her finger tips. As she reached in, the horse had raised one hoof slightly, and he had had to look away.

As the man finished his soda, a boy of eighteen or nineteen, the son of the stable owners, came in and sat down beside the girl and gave her a little hug. He watched the show for a minute, then began to unwrap the supper he had brought in a paper bag. He took out a banana, nudged her, and began drawing the skin back slowly. "Is this the way you like them?" he asked. She turned, looked at it a moment, then turned back to the television. "I've seen better," she said, and the boy laughed. She ignored him after that, and after he finished the banana and a sandwich, the boy rested his arm on the sofa back behind her, not touching her, and became engrossed in the show.

The riding ring was empty. The man left the club room, meeting the instructor coming in, who was talking to herself. He crossed the arena and found the farrier working on the woman's horse again, the woman beside him, speaking soft words of praise into the horse's soft-furred ear. The farrier was tired by now and talked even more, worked even more slowly, than before. He was telling the woman about the types of horse to watch out for: horses that have domed foreheads, that show a lot of white around the eyes, that are yellow in color.

The man leaned against a wall near them, numb now from waiting so long. The farrier was telling about a wild mustang he'd bought in Montana and brought back the year before. "That little filly looked so fierce," he said, squatting beside the patient horse, "the vet wouldn't go into the stall with him to give him his shots. I spent most half of fall building a stockade for breaking that son of a bitch. Nine foot high stockade. Finally I got some of my buddies over to help, and got the animal out into the stockade. I was scared to death, but then I just jumped on him bareback, like that Indian in Montana taught me. Expected to get thrown a mile. Well, damned if that bastard didn't act as calm as pie, went around that stockade like he was born in it, never bucked once. Hell, in a week the kids were riding him!" The farrier chuckled at his story, then turned to his work again. The woman, who was feeling relaxed and cheerful after the lesson, asked the farrier questions about everything he was doing. The man wondered if she thought the farrier was attractive.

He watched them for a while, then walked down the line of stalls. A huge, roman-nosed, gray stallion, a prize-winning jumper, was champing on a frayed, wet piece of wood he had torn from his stall. Curious, eyeing the man warily, the horse extended his massive head toward him over the gate of his stall as he passed. The man stopped, and the horse jerked back a little, nickering, letting the scrap of torn wood fall to the concrete floor of the passageway.

Feeling a sudden surge of compassion for the high-strung, powerful animal, a vague pity that nearly drew tears to his eyes, the man leaned over, and with two fingers he gingerly lifted the dark mass of pulped, sopping fibers, swung it once, and tossed it back into the stall. And the great gray horse startled, started back in his stall from whatever it was that was arcing suddenly towards him, reared, wild-eyed and screaming, pawing the ground and pounding his enormous, battering hooves against the boards of his stall in terror.

The Rules

DOWN IN THE COURTYARD, sparrows are feeding on the bread crumbs my landlady has thrown out to them after breakfast. They keep a few inches between them as they hop about nervously, first one hopping, then another, this way and that, one, two hops at a time, relationships constantly changing. It is like watching a complicated board game. I don't know the rules, but the movements of the small brown counters are swift and sure. The game moves along well, and I don't know the rules.

Submarine Warfare on the Upper Mississippi

THEY WOULD BE SURPRISED IF they knew we were here, they would be very surprised to know a German submarine hangs below the rippling surface of the Mississippi River, St. Paul to starboard, Minneapolis to port, they would be surprised. But here we are, a steel pike swimming almost motionless in the slow, young river, facing upstream.

How did we get here? That is what they would ask if they knew we were here. That would be their question, how did we get through the many locks, how did we slip past so many hostile eyes to come here, twelve hundred miles inland, to the "Land of Ten Thousand Lakes," to the "Land of Sky Blue Waters," how did we get here?

That is their question, it is not our question. It does not matter to us anymore, it is ancient history to us, it is "old hat." Their question is not our question. Our question is, what do we do now? Now that we have penetrated into the American State of Minnesota, an Unterseeboot of the VIIC Type, outmoded already when we sailed from Bremen, now that we are here, what do we do? That is our question, what do we do?

A prior question: why were we sent here? That is the question my First Mate asked. I had been fearing the question for a long time. What is our mission? I cannot tell him. I tell him, Willie, I cannot tell you that. You must not ask me the answer to that question.

He accepts this as if it had been an answer; he has faith in me and in the Admiralty. How can I tell him that I have not the smallest idea why we are here, why we were sent on this impossible journey, how can I tell him that, after all we have been through? That is my private question, how can I tell him? I do not know how.

The war is over for years, we know that. We are not idiots, we "know the score." The score is, Germany, 0; America, 2.

We know "what's up." The "jig" is up, we have known it for years.

So why have you not surrendered years ago, that is the question they would ask. The war is over for years, we don't even remember the war, what war? There has never been a war in the State of Minnesota, so what "gives"? Maybe you are part of the Sioux uprising? Maybe yours is a wild Indian submarine, ha, ha? That was our only war in Minnesota, and it was not even a war, an uprising is what it was.

We understand all this. We understand that our position, the attaining of it, the holding of it, is worse than pointless, it is ludicrous, and was so from before we, impossibly, attained it, a day we now know was fifteen days after the end of the Third Reich. We remember that day, twenty years ago, when we slid like a great savage pike between these cities, that is a day we remember, we will remember it when we have forgotten every other day. We are not stupid. We know the orders that we wait for will never come.

Today I have been talking with my First Mate, talking about the recent years, about what has come to break the monotony of this "waiting game" we hopelessly play. Not much, Herr Kapitän, he says. Willie, I say, you have it right, not much. The time we were trapped by the dredge, though, I say, that was a time, eh? That was a time, he says. We were against the American Army then, the Engineers. It was like the old days, slipping about along the bottom of the muddy river, alert always, backed further and further toward the terrible locks. It was a time, it was like the old days.

I thought then of retreating, after all these years, turning and running for the south, running for the Mexican Gulf, twelve hundred miles to the south, down the river we had forced twenty years before, forced like salmon. We will fail, Kapitän, my First Mate said. He had it right, we would have failed. We are not the men we were when we made that heroic voyage upcountry. The boat, she is not the boat she was, though we have done our best, oiling, greasing, scraping constantly, rebuilding, she is not what she was. We were magicians then, we and the boat, we could do anything, we could have sailed her up a garden hose. But not now. Willie had it right when he said that.

And so, with our propellors nearly over the dam, we made a run for it north, upstream, past the cow-like dredge, its big shovels and tangles of anchors leaving barely room for a good-sized carp. And we scraped a long and terrible sound along the web of cables and chains, the water was impossible, gravy, and we thought when we made that monstrous noise that we had "had it." But the watch must not have understood what was going on, and then nothing was, for we were past, free again in the newly scoured river bed, which we began to learn anew.

When the worst peril was past, when we were finally past, huddled under the pilings of the railroad bridge, we felt like men, then, our blood was flowing, and Willie, he was for sending our aft torpedo downstream into the dredging barge we had so carefully evaded, and I almost said yes, yes, though we could have done that more easily when we were facing it upstream. But I said nothing. The dredge finished its work in a few more days, and was towed away.

So we are still here. We have been here a long, long time; we have not been innocent guests. We are a steel lamprey between these two northern cities, locked in the ice during the terrible winters, rusting helplessly in the summer, we are a great parasite, we have no choice. We have made raid after raid to stay here, where we do not want to be, to stay alive, though we are not alive, to keep the boat living a little longer, which is rusting to death. We have stolen food and fuel, and killed those who prevented us. We make no excuse. We are at war, we are not trying to be loved. We are not children in a fairy tale, who the birds, maybe, feed. We take what we need, like the leech, and we will not be forgiven, no matter what, who have drifted in their midst like a horrible dream.

And Willie whispers to me in the darkness, Why? Kapitän,

why do we go on with this? And I tell him, Willie, don't ask, Liebchen, hush. A coal barge is passing slowly overhead. Our eyes in the darkness follow the sound of the pushing tug across our curving back. Let me sink it, he pleads, let me finish it. Not yet, my Willie, not yet, Kleine. We hug the steep curve of the sandbank, sheltering under the warning of the buoy, as we have learned to do.

We do not know why they have not found us yet, for we have made mistakes in spite of all our deep cunning. So that is another question, why have they not found us? Fishermen have seen us, old black men fishing from the quay, and lovers along the cliff-protected shore. But maybe lovers and fishermen keep what they know to themselves, being already whole. The deserters, one by one over the years, I have expected each of them to talk, needing to win favor. Each time one fails to return from a raid into one of these cities, then I think it is over at last, they will come for us now, blast us out of this bloody stream. But no. Perhaps they disappear, truly, once they determine to leave us, having lived so long like creatures in the underworld. Or maybe the strangeness of our existence is not something the mind can hold, and they forget like newborn babies forget their other life.

But we will reach the end. Not quite yet, Willie, Lieber, not quite yet. But soon; we will not have to wait for the rust to swallow us. For I saw him tonight, Willie. Lifting the hatch under cover of the bridge for a look around before light failed, Willie, I saw him watching us, writing it down in a book. Who? Saw who? Someone who writes it down, Willie, sitting on the edge of the pretty sandstone cliffs, prettily catching the last light of the day, watching us and writing it down. Willie, Willie, don't cry, Liebchen, it is what we knew would happen, what we have been terribly waiting for, all these years, Willie, there, soon we go home, there, there, Liebchen, soon now, soon.

WHEN I WAS ABOUT TEN I BUILT my first plastic model airplane, a Spitfire. A friend, several years older than I, came over to see it. I brought it out to the porch, where my friend waited, talking with my mother. My friend examined the plane and then observed that, instead of soaking the decal card in water and then ap-

Tact

plying just the thin film that floats off, I had cut the decals out, card and all, and attached them to the wings with glue. "I did that, too, the first time I built a model," my friend said.

Afterwards, my friend assured me that he had never, in fact, committed my blunder with the decals. "I just said that," he explained to me, "so your mother wouldn't think you're stupid." To this day I have appreciated his tact.

The Gardener's Story

AS HE KNEELED BEFORE A BED OF flowers, his fingers moving constantly, automatically through the foliage, pulling up a plant here, loosening the soil there, I leaned against my bicycle and we talked. "I've got an idea for a story for you," he said, his knees pressed into the moist, black earth, "a mystery. See what you can do with this. I'll tell you what the actual situation is, and you can take it from there."

"Fine," I said, watching him garden. "Shoot."

"This is true," he said. "Four years ago, when we first moved in here, people who thought we were Catholic informed us that we were in Immaculate Conception parish. A number of the kids in the neighborhood attend Immaculate Conception school, and the woman who lives next door teaches there. We see her leave every morning, she walks. On Sundays we can hear church bells that people say are from Immaculate Conception, and in the late summer and fall we hear a band practicing, which they say is from Immaculate Conception school."

Hah, I thought, I know what's coming. He straightened, trowel in hand, leaned backward to stretch the kinks from his back. Then he moved to a new, square-walled bed which I had helped him build. I helped with one version, at least; he has changed it many times since. I could recognize sections of the original, but most was strange, though seemingly long-established. The walls he builds look, within a few weeks, as if they've been there fifty years or more. He sets vines and mosses and little ferns into the earth-filled crevices, and they overrun the rough, scavenged stone, knitting the granite and limestone into a soft green web. Moss shadows the soft old brick of his herringbone walks and terraces almost as soon as he lays them, and they seem to have been there forever. And after he has raised or lowered the height of a terrace, changed the shape of a retaining wall, or moved a walled bed into a different part of the garden, the earth, the air, the patterning light settle almost at once, grow seamless and inevitable, denying they were ever otherwise.

Kneeling again, he began sifting through the already loose, fine soil, his fingers crushing marble-sized lumps of earth. As we talked, his hands never stopped moving. He saw me smiling. "You may have guessed," he said. "In all this time, in four years, none of us has ever seen Immaculate Conception church or school. I don't know where it is."

"Good," I said, spinning a pedal. "That's a good premise. Does it actually exist, that's the question. Now we just have to come up with a plot."

"There's the problem, of course," he said. "That's your job." As he began to spade at the base of a compost heap, carrying the dark, rich material over to a new bed he was putting in, I sat on the top tube of my bicycle, trying idly to balance sidesaddle.

"The real problem," I said, "is the common-sense objection to the premise. Why doesn't he, the protagonist, just ask someone for the street address of the church? Or, if he's embarrassed to admit he doesn't know where it is, why doesn't he look up the address in the phone book? Has the protagonist *tried* to find it?"

He looked puzzled. "Well, you'll have to work that out," he said. "You could find it in the phone book?"

"Sure," I said, "in the yellow pages, under 'Churches.'" I leaned my bike against the tall, vine-covered fence he had built around the garden and went over to look more closely at the profusion of flowers and herbs overflowing a stone-walled bed. When I asked him, he told me some of their names: delphiniums, periwinkle, phlox, nasturtiums, pinks. Comfrey, purple basil, mint, bee balm, parsley, dill. I sat on one of his stone benches in a shallow bower of arching lilacs. "This is a good place," I said.

"Isn't it though?" he answered. "Would you believe that the former owners had all the lilacs cut back? These all are volunteers."

"Volunteers," I laughed, struck by the word, and he smiled.

"For me it's not a metaphor," he said. "It's just what you call plants that spring up on their own." And he was a word man, too.

When I left, I rode a few blocks out of my way to go past what I assumed was Immaculate Conception church and school. It was not exactly where I had remembered it, though I have ridden past it many times. It was one street down, but it was there, big as life. Church, school, playground, parking lot — they took up a full block. I rode completely around it, but could find no name carved in the stone or set on a sign anywhere. But that must be Immaculate Conception, for the other churches in the area are clearly marked: Lutheran a block away, Seventh Day Adventist a block beyond that. And if there was no sign to prove that it was Immaculate Conception, and if there were no people around to ask at the moment I passed, still I have only to look it up to be sure. Yellow pages or white will do the job, once I get around to it. But what else could it be, a church and school of that size? If I could ever find the damn phone book when I want it I would look it up now. If I think of it, I'll ask someone, but really there's no doubt. What else could it be?

And so, I thought, there is no mystery. I thought, I will never write that story, for the story is not true for me, reality is too strong. Pretending will not change the facts, we have to deal in actuality or art will all decay into the arbitrary and the absurd. I thought, I know the kind of story that needs telling, the kind I want to write. I want to write simple stories about real life; the rest is child's play.

1 I LOVE THE GROCERY STORE

I GO INTO THE GROCERY STORE and look at the food, so cleverly arranged, the food and the non-food alike. It is nice and cool, and the aisles are almost empty now, so I push a cart before me, gliding through the almost empty aisles. I miss no display, nothing. I see

Three
Places

whether there is a new flavor of yogurt (there is: banana split with strawberry sauce); a new kind of paper towel (not today).

It is twelve o'clock noon, a traditional time for eating food, and a good time to look at it. Smoked mullets and ciscoes glisten like dark, oily gold in their plastic packages. The meat glows a fresh cherry red; fresh meat, fresh dye, who cares? I love the beautiful cans of Le Sueur peas; I love the veinèd cantaloupes.

One checkout clerk is very beautiful, and not very nice. She doesn't trust me, maybe because I come in so often, maybe because I buy almost nothing. "You work nights?" she asked me the other day, as I was paying for a small bar of soap which I had just wheeled up in a capacious cart. "Night and day," I tell her, "day and night." You see, it's mostly women you see in the grocery store in the middle of the day, and I am apparently male.

I would like her to think I am a consumer advocate, and so treat me with respect, almost with fear. But she won't be fooled. Consumer advocates, she knows, do not set the mousetraps in the mousetrap display, as she saw me doing last week. They do not come up to the checkout counter with an empty box of Keebler cookies, and two banana skins, and an empty milk carton, having eaten and drunk their respective contents on the spot. Consumer advocates do not have fits of gluttony, she knows that for sure. And she knows they do not, ever, stack cans of Little Friskies on the gourmet shelves.

So she is not very nice to me, however hard I try to win her over. She rings up my purchase sullenly, brutally, and she does not call out the price, however many times I stop her. She doesn't even ask me to have a nice day and thank me for shopping National, though a button on one of her nice breasts does. Still, I love the grocery store. It is what keeps me sane.

2

100% POLY

Another interesting place to spend some time is the fabric store. It is like a Kansas rube emerging from the subway into the heart of Harlem for a man to wander into a big fabric store for the first time. You see all ages there: little kids, old timers, teen-agers, the middle-aged; lots of people. It's like any place else. Except for one thing. You are the only male. Even the babies in the fabric store are female babies. You feel very funny, and you become very, very nonchalant.

I am after one square yard of unbleached muslin. That helps a little, for that is a good, honest, straightforward cloth. I need it for patching a fabric-backed antique map. A good, craftsman-like thing to do, I think. And I want suddenly to bolt, to tear out into the sunlight and shout to everyone who saw me enter the store, "I'm not going to sew anything, I'm going to *glue* that son of a bitch!"

But I don't, of course. No one saw me go in, neither do they give a damn. Do they think I'm not man enough to sew something, a button or something? I think maybe some good strong canvas might be the thing. Sailcloth. I think of the gnarled, nutbrown ancient mariner, mending sails with his

big steel needle. He pushes it along with hands that are like
leather hooks.

I stroll slowly through the store with a curious rolling gait,
looking for muslin or canvas or something of that sort, I'm
not particular. The funny thing is that although I am as con-
spicuous here as a buffalo among antelope, still no one can see
me. I discover this surprising fact after wandering about for
quite a while without one of these many women (who knows
which are clerks?) coming up to me and asking me if I need
help. Do I need help. I've just discovered that I am some kind
of eunuch here; I pose no threat, I offer no promise. Do I need
help.

I begin to look about systematically. There is every sort of
cloth except unbleached muslin. No bleached muslin, either,
for that matter. No canvas, no duckcloth, no sailcloth, no
fisherman's cloth. I wander over to some nice tweeds; I finger
them judiciously. My great grandfather was a tailor. I think I
may have inherited his feel for fabrics. A tailor at a military
academy in Faribault, Minnesota. I see a sign: 100% Poly.
Everything here is polyester. I am totally invisible, I nearly
panic again. Then I get curious about something.

In a few minutes a tall woman with glasses dangling upon
her breast from a ribbon asks me whether I need any help. She
asks quite loudly; it is possible this is the second or third time
she has asked, her voice has that quality. I am fingering some
nice polyester imitation wool plaid, although I am standing
deep in the territory of drapery fabrics, thirty-four yards
away. It is an impressive sight. "A third of a football field," I
tell her. She keeps her eyes on me. "Could you," I ask,
"show me something nice along the lines of an unbleached
muslin?"

3

AS YOU SEE ME TODAY

But the place that means the most to me, I have not been in it for many years, it may be gone by now, it probably is. The name is, or was, Sculpture Associates. It sounded to me like a Wall Street firm: Calder, Moore, Ray, Hepworth, and Smith, perhaps. It was an accident that I found it. Lost somewhere north of Greenwich Village, wandering with my roommate from the seminary and his sister in a beautiful region of warehouses of brick and little factories — electronics, cabinet making, hats — I saw the sign painted on the big plywood door and went in.

I often lag behind when I am walking with someone; my friends learn not to stop, not to look in the window or at the peculiar parked car with me, because then we will start moving backward after a bit, retracing our path. I don't understand it, it just happens, there's always something we missed, a little ways back. And so my roommate and his sister, after whom I carnally lusted, kept hurrying on, never noticed where I had disappeared, finally found the Village restaurant we were heading for, were pretty angry afterward. We never made it, my roommate's sister and I, until three years later, in Indiana.

Bigness. The place went up and up, back a mile. It could have held a house. But raw stone was what it held, it held row after packed cemetery row of dusty rough quarried stone, crazy, random shapes, and levels and layers of wood on wooden racks, twenty, thirty feet up. I didn't, don't know anything about stone, but the wood was no firewood: lignum vitae, butternut, teak, rosewood, hard mahogany, black walnut, boxwood, pear, cherry, I knew them. They were, the sawn logs, the crudely squared blocks, clouded like snakes

before molting, coated with paraffin like waterproofed, gro-
tesquely outsized matches. I look at my hand now, I can still
feel the wax packed under my nails that clawed across the flat
butt ends of ebony, oak.

Supplies for sculptors. Clay in barrels, 100-pound paper
cartons, standing sullen and uniform along one wall, WHERE
IS EVERYONE? the panic strikes, suddenly, for the first time
ever, out of nowhere in this barn on Seventh Avenue, SPEAK
TO ME! I shriek at the stone, SAY SOMETHING! to the
wood. No one is here, minding all this stuff. It's too heavy to
steal, but not heavier than color televisions, SAY SOME-
THING TO ME! I howl, I don't know what's happening to
me. A man's voice says something from the back of the building, then. Something dry slips out of my dry, twisted throat,
slips to the floor. I stare down at the dark foreign log my
hands clutch still, choked breathless.

"Sculpture supplies, I see," I say. The man looks at me.
"Need any help?" he asks then. He is holding a length of black
steel in his hand, silver tipped where its edge is being ground.
Along a side wall are ranks of gouges, black forged steel,
handled and unhandled, tangs like splinters of burned bone.
Rank after rank of specialized steel, graceful and dangerous,
cabinets of beautifully turned mallets, lignum vitae, maple,
shelves of rasps, modeling tools, clamps, vices, armatures,
four kinds of adze, I hadn't even seen them.

"Just looking," I say. "Need any help, just holler," he says
as he turns, returns to the grinding I can hear from some room
behind this great room. "Right," I say, "I'll holler." I wander
about the room when he is gone, touching everything, laying
hands on the cold stone, healing the scars my nails carved into
the wax of the wood, touching the shoulders of the forged,
razory tools. I cut myself on a mirror edge, bleed calmly into
my pocket, my abandoned blood gnaws soundlessly into the
perfect edge, perfect justice prevails for an instant.

I take the place in once more before I leave: the pulverizing
stone tools, the brilliant carving tools, the soft shaped model-

ing tools; the cutters, the drivers; the fast holders, the securers; the clay, the wood, the stone. As I leave, I bow down quickly and steal a small palm-sized piece of ebony from a crate of scraps. A pious man taking holy water after mass.

This was the store that changed my life. I did not become an artist, sculptor or otherwise. Not a thief, that was the first and the last thing I ever stole. Nor a dealer in wood or stone or any craft or art, nor salesman of any hardware. I did not become a teacher, any kind of shaper. You never know how these things will turn out. I became a fool, as you see me today. Don't ask me to explain, I won't, it can't be told. I will only tell you that what happened, happened in that slightly odd, yet ordinary enough place, and that I haunt, hunt all my waking, working hours for the place that will change me again.

HE HAS WRITTEN HER A ST. Valentine's Day love poem. It is very beautiful; it expresses, embodies a passionate, genuine emotion, emotion of a sort he hardly realized himself capable of, tenderness that is like the tenderness of a better man. At the same time, the imagery is hard, diamond clear, the form intricate yet unobtrusive. He says the poem out loud to himself over and over. He cannot believe it, it is so good. It is the best poem he has ever written.

Love Poems

He will mail it to her tonight. She will open it as soon as it arrives, cleverly timed, on St. Valentine's Day. She will be floored, she will be blown away by its beauty and passion. She will put it away with his other letters, loving him for it, as she loves him for his other letters. She will not show it to anyone, for she is a private person, which is one of the qualities he loves in her.

After he has mailed the poem to her, written out in his interesting hand, he types up a copy for his own files. He decides to send a copy to one of the more prestigious literary magazines, one into which he has not yet been admitted. He hesitates about the dedication, which could lead to embarrassment, among other things, with his wife. In the end he omits the dedication. In the end he decides to give a copy also to his wife. In the end he sends a copy also to a woman he knows in England, a poet who really understands his work. He writes out a copy for her, dedicated to her initials. It will reach her a few days late, she will think of him thinking of her a few days before St. Valentine's Day.

Bread Murder

"I'M GOING TO KILL SOMEONE with a loaf of bread," he says. He is alone. It is very late, it is two or three in the morning, and he is making a peanut butter and jelly sandwich. In honor of a friend whom he has not seen in a while he is making it in the manner of his friend: open-faced, on a piece of grainy whole wheat bread, a thick layer of peanut butter topped with a mound of black raspberry jam. The peanut butter is Deaf Smith, stiff from the refrigerator, uncooperative, rather than his altered and homogenized personal favorite. It gets seriously involved with his moustache and drips onto the table when he takes the first bite. It tastes okay, but not great.

And then the words come to him again, crystalline, irrefutable: "I'm going to kill someone with a loaf of bread." He seizes the loaf he was about to return to the refrigerator and rushes out into the hallway of his apartment building. Mrs. Garvey, his neighbor, is passing by. He brings the sturdy loaf down on her egg-frail old head, a death blow. Crumbs explode. He looks around. No one is there. Mrs. Garvey is in bed, it is two or three in the morning. He returns to his apartment and reflectively finishes his p.b.j.

Four days later the idea that he will perpetrate an homicide with a loaf of bread has not left him. His apartment is bakery full of bread: whole wheat, cracked wheat, rye, pumpernickel, many kinds of white. He squeezes a loaf of Wonder Bread between his hands. Mrs. Garvey next door is listening to one of an endless series of shrill daytime quiz shows. Her bird-like hands flutter up suddenly, there is a muffled cry, the plastic loaf molds itself to her face, she slumps onto the runner before her sofa. He stuffs the loaf of bread under his coat. It retains the startled impression of Mrs. Garvey's face.

He gives a lecture that evening on the evolution of the ideal of originality in Western Culture. His small and inattentive audience stifle yawns and sneak glances at their watches. Be-

hind him, in his briefcase, there is a startled peanut butter and
jelly sandwich: Peter Pan Creamy, Welch's Grape, Wonder
Bread.

I'm Sorry That You're Dead

"THAT'S RUBBISH," MY UNCLE says, "that's just bunk." And my grandmother tells him, "Hush now, shut up," and he shuts up. "Thank you," I say to her and continue my explanation. We had gathered in my apartment to begin the trip back to the lakes in northwest Minnesota that were my family's fishing lakes sixty years before. We are using an old map, old sixty years ago, a huge map of oilskin that hangs in my study taking up half a wall, floor to ceiling, an 1883 map of Minnesota and edges of Dakota, Dominion of Canada, Wisconsin, and Iowa. It is detailed, cross-hatched mile by square mile, except for Indian Lands, which are mostly blank, unceded.

Most of us are dead; that is the only way we could all squeeze into the little room. Even so, it is crowded, and my grandfather complains. He was a crotchety, irascible man. "Keep your shirt on," I tell him, "we'll be out of here in a few minutes." He takes a slow swing at me with the patent, spring-loaded gaff he has been carrying around, along with his newspaper-wrapped casting rod, ever since getting off the train. He has had the gaff for many years, and keeps its four incurving steel talons razor sharp and the spring steel oiled. Landing nets are unreliable, he says, effete.

Vergus, the town we are heading for, is about two hundred miles from St. Paul, an easy four or five hour trip on modern highways. But there are for us only a series of very bad roads, following the Mississippi north to Fort Ripley, then northwest, roughly following the Northern Pacific Railway. The map, of course, is thirty years older than we need, but it is all I have. The roads hadn't changed much in that short time, I argue, but my uncle is disgusted. He has always thought me soft-headed. But there is no other way. Besides, everyone over sixty, those alive and those dead, believe they remember the way.

It took us thirteen hours, including a picnic on the church lawn of one of my grandfather's old seminary classmates, and frequent stops for repairing the tires on the Model T, and many wrong turnings, before we arrived. It was a good trip, though, and my tiny, fierce grandmother kept everyone in line, the living and the dead, those present and those away; it makes no difference to her. She had seen an angel once, it had appeared to her during the tornado that mashed flat their parsonage and church in Omaha, and ever since she has been able to stand up to anyone. She could before, too.

Everyone finally in bed after the long drive, my grandfather studies me as we sit at the oilcloth-covered table in the big cabin. I am still wearing the broad-brimmed felt hat that had annoyed everyone so much in the crowded car. My hair, uncut for a long time, curls out like a brush fire. My fingers comb restlessly at my beard as I try to get some writing done. "You look like a fool," my grandfather says, still angry at me.

I put down my pencil. "I am a fool, Grandpa," I say. You talk pretty straight to a man who has been dead for nine years. He gives his high, pleasant laugh.

"Well, my boy," he says, adjusting his gold-rimmed glasses on his gaunt face, "at least you're honest. And there are worse things than being a fool. As Paul says, we are fools for Christ's sake." Meaning St. Paul, in Corinthians.

"Grandpa," I say, "you and St. Paul may be fools for Christ's sake, but I'm afraid I'm just plain a fool, for chrissake." I laugh, hoping he will appreciate the little joke, which in fact is my father's little joke, from his seminary days.

"Well," he says. "Well, well, well." His hawk's face and straight, still-dark hair and metal-rimmed glasses nod over the table at me. We are having a little of his favorite brand of California port, very cheap. "Well," he says, "well, well, well." Elastic bands above his elbows keep his sleeves the proper distance up his skinny, liver-spotted wrists. Finally he smiles a little, a small, cracking smile. Then he frowns again. "My boy," he says, "at least take off that blasted hat."

And when we arrived in Vergus we were coming from the north, from Manitoba, from an anniversary celebration at the church my grandfather had started in 1902. The church was in Landestreu. Landestreu, meaning faithfulness to the land, a name changed by war wisdom in 1914 to MacNutt. "From Landestreu," he says, the word cradling on his tongue, "to MacNutt!" two hard, wart-like syllables. "Oh my, oh my, oh my," he sighs. "Oh my, oh my," shaking his sad hawk's face. In World War I, when his brother Paul, a runaway, wildman living alone in a shack in the Canadian wilderness, was made a Mountie to patrol against German invasions. Such as my grandfather, who one time made the trip north, alone, to check on his brother, and was arrested as a spy at the border. "Oh my, oh my, oh my." Paul, drafted into the Royal Canadian Mounted Police, whose only companion was a big dog named Bismarck.

For we had heard the fishing was good around Vergus, on Loon Lake, famous for bass, and thought we could rent a cabin from someone. "SCHATTSCHNEIDER, THE GERMAN BUTCHER," said a sign when we first came into town, and that's where we went, and he set us up on Sybil Lake (no cabins on Loon, then), in a very primitive cabin. Schattschneider, who bartered eggs and bacon and butter for our gunnysacks of surplus fish, which went to his smokehouse, which has outlived Schattschneider.

And the first morning my grandfather and Walter, the oldest, went off to Loon to get the big bass there, leaving behind Ewald and my father. We seined some minnows, E. and I, and pushed out in the old, rotting boat that came with the cabin. Afterwards we showed him our gunnysack, as heavy as his, but not with bass. "Pa," we asked, "what are these fish with the great eyes?" He took one long look, struck his forehead with his hand, and announced with reverence in his voice that the fish with the great eyes was the walleyed pike, about which nobody had bothered to tell him. "The walleyed pike," he said, arranging them one by one on the still-wet morning grass beside the dock, "is the finest eating fish on this earth. Equalled, perhaps, by the great northern pike. To which it is not related, as you can see."

"Grandpa," I plead, "sit down. Dad says I have to row in if you start standing up." He glares at me from the back of the flat-bottomed boat, rocking gently, his antique steel casting rod poised in one hand, the other fingering a sopping cigar butt. Ancient preacher's coat hanging long and loose on his stroke-racked frame.

Once, when my father was still-fishing at age five, he flukishly hooked a big northern which his cane pole somehow held until it could be secured with the new patent gaff. Now, my grandfather was not one to display his catch; it was nobody's business what he was bringing up, which could lead to other questions, and then encroachment on favorite spots. He kept his fish in wet gunnysacks, and the world saw nothing but lumpy burlap and a particular degree of strain in the arm carrying it. But the boy pleaded, and was surprisingly allowed to carry the northern up, dangling from a piece of rope. Two city fellows, elaborately tackled, met the child and fish climbing up from the dock, the fish as long as the child, and asked him where he had gotten it. They knew better than to ask his pa. The boy answered, in German, "Der liebe Gott hat ihn mir gegeben," and his pa, poker straight, translated for the blank-faced city fellows, "He says the good Lord has given it to him."

"I mean it, Grandpa, I promised, dammit." Almost in tears. The language is acknowledged and ignored. The old man sits down with a snort. "Well, then, get us in closer." He gestures angrily toward the weedline; relieved, I work the boat in carefully. The rod comes back in its great sidearm sweep, I dodge, the monstrous triple-jointed plug flies out toward the scalloped, heavy line of lilies, lands with a crash several inches from the table of flat green.

We ate together every evening that summer. The bowl of steaming pink soup passes down our long table, our two picnic tables set up outside. This is The Fish Soup, the one real fish soup, my grandmother's grave-held secret, unduplicated since. A good chance to finally get that recipe, I think, and am about to ask her for it, but she goes into the cabin to get something. Heads of great northern pike were in it, that we know. The bowl is passed to me. An eye floats up, looks at me flatly. The child leaves the table, is sick behind the cabin, leaning against a birch tree.

My father and his brothers get up very early to reach the narrows before first light. Too young, too old, we listen to their preparations, and go out ourselves after the sun is almost up. "Promise me. Or you can't go out. Don't let Pa stand up, come in if he starts. Watch his backswing. And wear a hat. And don't overtire yourself, take it easy. You're taking your pills, aren't you?" Because of his stroke the winter before. Because of my "fainting spells." Because of all that waiting to break loose in our heads again.

"You and I," he said once, tapping his glasses after I had first appeared with mine, monstrous, "we are weak-eyed but very smart. Smarter than any of them, you and I." But all that hell, those two species of hell, there, waiting to knock us silly again.

There was one summer, on Sybil, when the walleyes grew to enormous proportions, and would bite on nothing but little green frogs, which were abundant then: cold wet locusts on the shore. After we had filled two gunnysacks the old man sat back; addressing the blue mid-morning sky in his great preacher's voice he asked, "When will this unprecedented slaughter cease?" Not that summer, though no one else caught much. They would watch us, from a decent distance at first, then gradually move toward us in their boats as we caught fish after fish, until finally we had barely room to throw out our lines. But it wasn't the spot, it was the frogs, which no one could believe. It ceased later, though.

And when we went into town to buy provisions or go to church, Pa would stop to talk to a man emptying trash cans or shoveling horseshit and would talk for fifteen minutes about how much horseshit accumulates per day in a town of that size, depending on the season, and how long the man lived there, and were his folks from around here, and what did they do, and who was the mayor and who was the best barber. And we would say, "Pa, come *on,* dammit, we want to get back and go swimming," though not, of course, so he could hear us. He found out some funny stuff. He learned that the local name for the big, blue-gray wading birds we saw stalking along the water's edge was "shikepoke," and spent hours in the library when he got back to Omaha, and later he wrote me with indignation that shikepoke was a variant of shitepoke, from the bird's practice of defecating when startled — a disrespectful name, he thought, for the great blue heron, which was what the bird was. It was always the great blue heron, the largemouth and the smallmouth black bass, the great northern pike, the muskellunge. They were lords, they deserved their proper names.

In a fishhouse, twenty-two years later, cleaning fish, a man remembered him. "Your grandpa always carried his fish up in gunnysacks," that's what he remembered. "He was a hell of a fisherman."

He was. And that day he and I caught five bass over three pounds, though we had gotten out late, and my father and uncles came in with just one bass and a pair of hammer-handle northerns. My father laughed hard about that, and my Uncle E. was too disgusted to speak.

This is northern water we are in now: a long, sharp point of pickerel reeds on a submerged sand bar that extends far out into the lake. Grandpa sits in the back, bent forward, tying on a long wire leader, to which he snaps a battle-scarred, triple-jointed wooden minnow. "It's a little late for northern here," I say. He continues his operations in silence, tying a triple knot, testing it savagely, then stands up shakily to cast.

"My boy," he says, "you can never tell. You can never tell." He says it, as always, in a high, chanting voice, and

repeats it at odd moments, like the one remembered phrase of
a good song. "You can never tell."

"Why don't you stay down, Grandpa; I can get her in
closer," I say, but he remains as he is and begins the great
sidearm backswing that brings the armory of treble hooks
perilously close to my ear, then snaps it forward. There is, of
course, no reason to argue with him about it any more. It was
his heart that got him, finally, not the old enemy, stroke. But
habit is a part of love and lives along with it stubbornly.

I sit at the oars, and watch the old wrists twitch the plug
through the tall, slim reeds. There is an explosion, a good one,
a northern's long body, green, white bellied, going berserk,
trying to dig now into the bottom weeds, he whoops crazily
and jerks the square steel rod back, doubled against the pike,
skinny arms straining out of the floppy coat, reel screeching
against his oblivious smoking thumb. And slowly he makes a
little headway, working him in a little. I have the oars in, the
landing net already in the water, and he screams, "The gaff!
Use the gaff!" and I think maybe he's right, it's too long for
the net, so I cock the damn thing, spreading its curved talons
till they gape open in a line, but I'm not sure exactly where to
hit him and he's going to be lively when he sees the boat, and
so I drop the cocked, dangerous gaff and go for him after all
with the net, digging deep into the water as he brings him
around, turns his head into the net, and I scoop him out, keep
him diving into the mesh, his long thick body half out and
drop him tangled into the boat's bottom.

We sit there a moment, staring down at the fish still thrash-
ing on the wooden slats. Thirteen, maybe fifteen pounds,
thick as an anaconda. My grandfather's mouth works
strangely, then he realizes what is wrong, and spits out the
chewed-off cigar and reaches into his coat for a fresh one. His
dark mottled skinny hands are shaking a little. I begin warily
to untangle the crocodile-dangerous northern and the mass of
hooks from the knotted cords of the net. We are both laugh-

ing and talking nonsense at once. "Hot damn," I say, "hot damn."

The serious fishing of the morning over, my father leans back and laughs till there are tears in his eyes. He is telling stories about his seminary days, and his rough boyhood in Omaha, and his Uncle Paul, who became a sort of mountain man on the Canadian prairie, who had to leave home after blasting his old man's prized crystal doorknob off the door of their outhouse, hit it with a twenty-two from a block away, his old man crapping inside. He laughs so hard he cannot talk, the boat rocks, we don't care if we catch anything more that morning.

"Grandpa," I say to him, hoisting the heavy, rope-tied burlap bag over the edge of the boat. It hangs there cool and dark, the murderous fish curved inside. "Grandpa," I say to him, "I'm sorry that you're dead." He leans forward, cups his thin hands against the wind, lights his cigar in the brief flash of the match. Then he looks at me narrowly, sun glinting off his fragile glasses. He grips the worn cork handle of his rod, sets his thumb on the reel of wet black line. We have drifted down the reed line. He studies the line of reeds, notices a pocket, a little bay in the line of reeds. He stands up, and I steady the boat for him.

Entry

THEY ARE SITTING BESIDE EACH other on the edge of her bed, quiet, their arms around each other, murmuring to each other from time to time in low, exhausted voices. Both have been crying, or have been held at the edge of tears by the intensity and difficulty of their raw-nerved, night-long talk. They are emotionally drained, but happy, having finally resolved, torn away finally what has long been a razor between them. Their hands have long come away bone sliced, tendon severed, when either reached out to the other.

Now that is gone, they have beaten, bloodied their way through it tonight, it will be all right between them again, they have never been closer. He kisses her tenderly, rises; he goes to the bathroom. When he returns, she is writing in a notebook and does not look up when he returns. Something cold and heavy crawls into his stomach and settles there. She loves him more than he will ever love her.

DURING THE SUMMER OF THE
Bicentennial the Freedom Train
came to the small town in central
Illinois where my mother and
father live. It came to their town,
and passed through, but it did not
stop. It was not scheduled to stop;
they knew it would not, for the
town is too small. It would stop
when it reached Peoria, twenty
miles to the west. My mother told me about it.

Waiting for the Freedom Train

A week or more in advance the newspaper carried a story of
the Train, along with its schedule. It would be coming from
Chicago, along an old Illinois Central line which had carried
nothing but freight for many years. The line passes right
through my parents' town. From the porch of their house you
can hear, can feel the freight trains that rumble through from
time to time. One train comes through fairly regularly about
two in the morning; people hear it only when they are having
trouble getting to sleep, and then the low sound is as lonely as
death. There is usually no reason for these trains to stop here,
and they rarely do.

The paper said that the Freedom Train would pass through
at five-thirty P.M., and that it would slow down and blow its
whistle. It was a convenient time. Except for the local shop-
keepers, the men and women of my parents' town mostly
work at the Caterpillar plant in Peoria. Caterpillar has a night
shift, but most people would be home.

Everyone in town knew about the Train, and they talked
about it often, though there was little you could say about it,
except that it was coming, and that you were looking forward
to it. It contained reproductions, the paper said, of the nation's
most precious documents, and many original items of histori-
cal importance or general interest and national pride. The suit
Robert Redford wore in *The Sting*. Jack Benny's violin.

The Train was scheduled to come through at five-thirty; by
five o'clock people had begun to drift down to the open area
behind the cement plant — the best place in town to watch

trains. It was a fine August afternoon; the worst heat of the day was over.

My mother was canning tomatoes as the time approached, and she did not especially want to interrupt her work for what was, after all, just a train. But my father, who has more sense of history, said it was a once-in-a-lifetime experience, and that they should not miss it. And so she took off her apron, and they walked together the few blocks down to the tracks.

Most of the town was gathered by the tracks or on the several lawns that overlook the yard of the cement plant and the crossing. People were standing around, many with cameras, or sitting on the stacks of bricks or red tile drainage pipes, and children were climbing the big, eroded mounds of sand and gravel. People kept glancing at their watches and stared down the tracks, and parents nervously snatched their children out of the way when they began to play on the tracks.

But the Train was not in sight yet at five-forty-five. By six there was a definite, though low-keyed, air of anxiousness, for it was supper time, and past, for most of the town. Two families, relative newcomers, had brought picnic dinners, which they were spreading self-consciously on a sloping lawn. But most of the people in this town, like my father and mother, like to eat at a table.

By six-thirty families had begun to hurry home in small groups to catch hasty suppers, to fill a thermos with lemonade or coffee, and hurry back. In several cases, the older children stayed by the tracks, keeping watch, while their parents took younger sisters and brothers home for supper. A carload of high school and past high school kids squealed off to the local drive-in and soon returned with provisions for the larger group that clustered off by themselves. My mother says that my father kept listening fearfully for the whistle while he ate, and he would not even wait for coffee.

Almost everyone was back by seven, relieved that nothing

had happened while they were gone. The sentinels reassured them again and again. As the sun dropped, the evening took on a bit of a chill, but most had taken advantage of the trip home to grab a sweater or light jacket. Everyone sat on blankets, and waited.

It grew dark about nine. The Train had not come by nine-thirty. It had not come at ten. By this time children were asleep in their parents' arms; people talked in low voices. The high school group had gotten some beer someplace and had moved farther off down the tracks, but they were subdued and drank quietly and discreetly, and nobody bothered them.

After it grew dark a few families reluctantly drifted home, but most stayed. "After waiting such a long time," my mother said, "it did seem sort of a shame to miss it after all. Still, I was ready to go, but not Dad." The few people who left said they thought they might go into Peoria the next day and actually go through the Train, would pay their money and take a ride on the conveyor belt past the displays. My mother doesn't know that anyone did.

It was past ten-thirty when the Train finally appeared. The paper the next day explained that there had been mechanical problems back fifteen or twenty miles that had caused the delay. After the Train passed through my parents' town, there was another sort of delay: the citizens of Washington, a town somewhat larger than my parents' town, forced the Train to stop for a while by putting flares on the tracks.

Nobody in my parents' town thought of doing that, though my mother almost wished they had. People had long since stopped stepping out onto the railbed to peer down the tracks, and so the Train was almost upon the town before anyone realized it. Children were woken hurriedly, some crying, as the unfamiliar chuffing grew louder and the great white headlight swung into sight. The Train did not slow down much as it approached the crossing and loomed up over the people squinting into its sudden glare; it was apparently trying to make up a little for the lost time. But the whistle did blow once as the big engine and the cars it pulled pounded past in the darkness.

In less than a minute the Freedom Train was out of sight again. After a few minutes of gazing down the empty track, the people of the town gathered up still half-asleep and sleeping children, and said good night to each other in quiet voices, and went home.

IT WAS GOING TO BE A RUSHED and complicated morning, at best, but it had started well. I had managed to catch the right bus, and the chances were good that I could stick to my schedule: get off at the bank, cash a small check, catch another bus the rest of the way downtown, make several necessary purchases, and then

The Milwaukee Poets

take still another bus back to school in time for my early afternoon class. My lecture notes were in my briefcase; I would finish working on them during the return trip. That was the next-to-last item on my list: finish lecture notes before class. The last item was: teach class.

About six blocks from the bank we stopped to let on a young man who had been waiting on a corner. He seemed somehow familiar when he boarded the bus and sat down across the aisle from me. I thought at the time that he might be a graduate student; he was about that age, I thought, and wore an old army jacket. That was the way he disarmed my usual aloofness. But I had no idea where we might have met, if ever, and I might have been merely reflecting the look of recognition he seemed to give me. As it turned out, we had never met, though he was as well-known to me as a brother.

When he got on, I was checking my list, adding a few tasks which I had already accomplished, but hadn't written down. After he sat down, the young man looked at me curiously for a few blocks, and then asked, "Don't you teach at St. Thomas?"

I said that I did.

"Tell me," he said then, "what do you think about the Milwaukee poets?"

"What Milwaukee poets?" I asked. To my knowledge I didn't know any poets in or from Milwaukee, much less have any thoughts about them.

But instead of explaining which poets he had in mind, he asked me, "You're Jonathan Sisson, aren't you?"

"No," I said, "I know him, though. He's a friend of mine."

"But don't you teach at St. Thomas?"

"Yes," I said, "so does Jon." He looked dissatisfied. "We both teach at St. Thomas," I said, "Jonathan and I. At St. Thomas. We both teach there." He looked at me. "Jonathan may know about the Milwaukee poets," I suggested, feeling unaccountably, appallingly diminished by my ignorance of them.

"He taught at Indiana last year, didn't he?"

"Jonathan?" I said. "No, *that*'s me. At least, I taught there a few years ago, when I was in graduate school."

"And you published a book with another guy?"

"No," I said, "that was Jonathan, with two other guys."

He looked at me with narrowed eyes.

"Jonathan has a beard too," I said, "and wears glasses. That's probably what confused you, we poets all look pretty much alike." I laughed.

He looked at me with narrowed eyes, then glanced out the window. "Jesus Christ, you nearly made me miss my stop," he said, and pulled frantically at the bell cord.

"See you later, Jon," he said as he pushed out the back door of the bus. "I'll stop over some time." And then he was gone.

I sat dully for a few minutes, then realized we were a long way past the bank. The stop I had almost made him miss was my stop, too.

At this point it was too late to get off and go back; I did not really regret it. For I now realized who the young man was, and I was grateful to be at least temporarily quit of him. I continued on the bus downtown and wandered aimlessly for an hour or so, ending up at the Robert Street bridge. I stood there for a while, trying to get a hold on myself, thinking of the person on the bus.

Though I had heard his voice many times, I had never before met him face to face, and it was that that had upset me. For years he has been calling me on the phone, pretending that I am someone else, usually someone I do not even know. He asks sometimes whether a particular woman is here, and I think for a moment it is some jealous husband or boyfriend. I do not know which rattles me more, when he asks for someone whom I once knew very well, but have not seen in years, or when he asks for total strangers.

It is always after I hang up that I realize who the caller was, and then I feel chilled, wasted, weak. And that was who it was who was on the bus. And now I have met him face to face, and it is much worse than it was. He is the One Who Brings Confusion. I believe in no other devil.

Cello

HE PRACTICES ON THE CELLO most of the night. She is pregnant. She once played the cello, too, that's how they met, in the orchestra, but not now, she never plays now, she stopped when she became visibly pregnant, though it is common now to continue with what you are doing until almost the last minute, especially if you are an artist. "You play enough for the two of us, now," she says to her husband. It is true, he plays most of the night.

It is as if she had swallowed her cello, she thinks, as she stands naked before a mirror, her legs awkwardly astraddle. She turns away. She draws her hand across her tight belly, makes a sound that is nothing like the sound of a cello. The sound of a cello creeps up the stairs, as if apologetic, from where her husband is practicing. "You're playing for two, now," she says, "remember." He plays most of the night.

The Bicycle That Went Mad

IT WAS A WRONG ONE, I COULD tell that at once, but I couldn't explain it. There was nothing of the usual sort you could complain about in its materials or even in the workmanship. All that was the best, most expensive you can get. It fit him, and the frame's steep angles were right for the bike's one purpose: sprint track racing. I file my lugs a little smoother, a little thinner, but nobody else around here does that kind of work. This was not a problem of sloppy workmanship. By almost every standard the bike was fine, better than most imports.

But when he first showed it to me out at the old fairgrounds velodrome on that sweltering August morning, I knew something about it was very, very bad. I thought at first that there might be something twisted about its chain stays — nothing obvious, something only a trained eye would pick up. However, when I got down and checked them with a tape and calipers (everybody told me I was crazy), they were absolutely accurate. I had him let me ride it a few laps; it ran perfectly true, even in the sharp, steep turns. Even so, for some reason I was sweating and shaking when I got off. I dismounted on the far end of the infield to try adjusting a few things before returning it to him. I *knew* the bike was wrong. I just couldn't explain it.

Ernie had spent two months' pay on it, I knew that, so I didn't have the heart to press my suspicions any farther — God knows now I wish that I had. Al Macready built it for him. I was originally going to, but didn't have enough free time, as it turned out. I work real slow and he was in a hurry. Macready is relatively new to frame building — when I built my first frame he was still using training wheels — but usually he does good work. He went wrong this time, though. I don't blame him — strange things just happen sometimes.

Ernie had taken the overall state track championships the year before, still a junior, and this year he was considered an

Olympic possibility. Around here, Mikkleson was his only competition in the matched sprints. But as we worked through the long series of matches and *repêchages*, starting before noon, running through the terrible heat of the afternoon (I rode for the hell of it, as usual, and was dropped as soon as you'd expect of an old man), you could see that Ernie was dissatisfied. After each race he got off and fussed around the bike instead of resting.

Not that he needed rest. He won his early matches without any trouble, not even bothering with the usual jockeying and stalling for position. He'd just wait until the final lap and then ride away from everyone with that incredible kick of his. You couldn't jump away from him, either; he was too quick, too strong.

After his semi-final race he dismounted, flipped the bicycle over roughly, borrowed my tool box, and, with me helping, began checking every damn thing you could think of — chain tension, bearing adjustment, various alignments. I myself checked his tires to see that they were well-glued, for he said he sensed one of them might roll. He couldn't really explain what he had felt, any more than I could; it was something like a grabbing and something like an unsteadiness, but really neither of these. We checked everything, then checked again. It seemed perfect. I don't think I'll ever again trust any bike I haven't built myself.

Ernie's last race, the only one that was in any doubt, was about to begin. I urged him to use my bike (we're about the same height and build). It's nothing flashy, but it's straight as hell and holds no unpleasant surprises. I built it, and I know what I know. Besides, he could have won on a tricycle, he was so good.

But he'd have none of it. He claimed it was all in his head, even got a little angry at me for planting the idea that something was wrong. He rode a practice lap and everything felt all right, he said. Very ill at ease, I stepped out on the track — I was holding for him then. I held him steady and, at the gun, gave him a good, even push.

He blew his rear tire almost immediately. That's not unusual, of course, considering the terrible pressure they carry and the rough shape of that old track. But those were new, well-aged tires. I helped him put in his spare wheel, but then that tire blew too. That should have settled it for me. I should have used force, if necessary, to keep him from riding on that bicycle. Instead I loaned him one of my own wheels, even put it in for him.

As he slowly pedaled up to the starting line again, I caught him and held him steady for still another try. And then I saw something that I'll probably never get over. As I gripped his saddle frame to hold him upright for the start, the seat- and chain-stays holding that rear wheel, my own wheel, suddenly distorted, warped themselves an instant like something seen through rough water, then straightened again as if nothing had happened. I was apparently the only one who saw it; Ernie, even, seems not to have felt it. But I saw it and my knees nearly gave way. I suddenly felt sick with dread, and dizzy, all in that instant. The starter's gun fired just then and Ernie pulled away from my now slack grip. He glanced back for a second to try to see why I hadn't given him a push, why I'd given him such a wobbly start. If only I'd hung on like a rivet.

Mikkleson was waiting for him, and they moved off together slowly while I prayed, without hope, for another flat. They pulled away slowly, Ernie allowing Mikkleson to drop behind. I could see he was still fretting a little as they rounded the first, steep turn, high up on the bank. But then he seemed to forget his mechanical problems. We could see him start to play with Mikkleson, giving little false jumps and feints toward the pole. But Mikkleson wouldn't go for it. He's smart, though he has none of Ernie's power. They say he's pretty upset over this whole business.

Ernie finally made his move off the top of the last turn, dropping down the bank like a rock, giving it everything for the first time that day. Mikkleson hung on desperately, knowing that once he lost Ernie's wheel he was finished.

For all Mikkleson's work, Ernie steadily widened a gap, and it all seemed to be over. Then Ernie and his bike shuddered, like, for an instant. I saw it plain as I'm standing here. In that instant Mikkleson lunged into his draft again, hung there for a moment, then moved to the outside to go around, his face a red mask of effort.

Ernie was scared then, they were close enough you could see it on his face, but he wasn't scared of Mikkleson. No one knew what must have been twisting around inside him. Even his body didn't know, which kept straining ahead.

It was when they were five yards from the finish, heads down between straining arms, legs pumping into a blur, neck veins nearly bursting, the crowd shouting at the unexpected challenge, that it finally happened. I was watching, I was closer than anyone, and I saw what I saw. People claim that Mikkleson's pedal hit Olson's chain and that that was what snapped it, but I saw what I saw.

They were close, but there was clear space between the two when that chain parted. It parted of its own self, I can see it still, like in slow motion, snapped *below* the chain wheel, not where there's tension, on top, snapped below and swung up like a buggy whip and wrapped itself in a flash around poor Ernie's straining neck and jerked down under the force of his still pumping legs and broke his neck like a sparrow's.

I saw what I saw. And while they were pushing and shouting and trying to untangle the poor devil, past help already, I knew what I had to do. I dragged that machine off the track, its fork warped now into an insane twist, and in the coldest and most rational moment of my life I lifted it above my head and smashed it again and again down onto the baked ground of the infield, smashed it beyond a rumor of repair.

As they dragged me away from it, its glowing, pearly finish went dull and flat, fading to a chalky dead white.

They told you I was crazy, didn't they? Well, I saw what I saw. I know what I know. That bicycle was as mad as the moon.

A Regular Old Time Miser

"SHIT," HE SAID, WIDE-EYED, "you're a regular old time miser!" "Damn right, sonny," I answered him. The pretty pennies and nickels and dimes and quarters filtered through my sifting fingers like rich, thick sand. He was only twelve years old, the son of my best friend, and could not be expected to completely understand. He knew, however, what he knew.

A regular old time miser, that's what I am. Meaning that I care nothing for prosperity, but that I love money, the actual, fleshy, legal tender, filthy lucre, coin and currency alike. I'll be blunt: it gives me an erection to touch the lovely stuff, to smell its brazen scent, to see the light strike the complex planes and smooth and fluted curves, to listen to the sweet bells of their jingling ring together, to taste, ah, their matchless, public taste: an old nickel smooth on the tongue, the jawbreaker half dollar, the rapid mouthing of a pocket-softened fiver.

Yes, there you cringe, turn slightly pale. There you are shocked a little, you jaded libertine, there you shudder, sophisticate. All right, say the worst, say it is excrement. You, passionate lady, what do you take into your eager mouth? And you, gentleman, where do you put your lapping tongue?

Now you are beginning to understand, to see finally what that child, son of my best friend, saw at a glance. But no, to be honest, probably it was the superficial aspects of the scene that did it for him — a certain pose: the sensual slump over the heaped glory; a certain sound: the involuntary cackle, the jingling of the finger-sifted coins — that caused him to connect me with the stock description. And thus his understanding must be superficial; yours might be deeper.

But do you understand? Do you recognize now that those ancients you read about in the paper and shake your head over, those old geezers in flophouses, those crones in weed-surrounded shacks who are discovered, weeks dead, too skinny to stink, lying on mattresses fat with fortunes in cash, do you recognize in them, now, not miserable lunatics but the luckiest of lovers, faithful to the end? That when you say, "What a shame! How pathetic! If only he had put some of that dough to work, invested it, spent it, given it away!" that then I answer, "How tragic! How sad! If only he had prostituted his wife, sold his children, sent his lovely mistress screaming to a nunnery!"

For the love of money is the beginning of wisdom, and where a man's treasure is, there will his heart be also. And that is what that boy, blundering in on me, looking for his mother and discovering a cliché come fascinatingly to life, that is what he looked at but was too young to understand. And that is what you, sexual athlete, you, charitable lady, you, Good Samaritan, will certainly fail to see: that we misers, we real old time misers, are the only real lovers, loving with a pure and burning passion; that the truest love is the love that can never be returned; and that in loving our gold, copper, silver, crinkling paper, it doesn't matter, money, we are like unto God, for we love what we have made, and what we have made loves nothing at all, for that is the way we have made it.

The Wish-Fulfillment Camera

I WAS HAVING LUNCH WHEN George came in and showed me the photographs. He owns the camera shop across the street from the library, and we often have lunch together. He sat down across from me in the booth, pushed my plate a little to the side, though I was only half done, and set the envelope of prints in front of me, all without saying a word.

"What are these?" I asked, a little petulantly, and made no move to touch the envelope. I had had a rather unpleasant misunderstanding with Miss Gloria Epsom that morning and therefore was not in a generous mood. You know Gloria?

"Just look at them," he said, "and tell me what you think." He was obviously agitated and kept pushing the prints toward me in little impatient shoves. Finally I wiped my hands on a napkin, put on my glasses, and began glancing through the set, rapidly at first, then more slowly. I laid the prints down carefully on the envelope when I was through.

"I'm no expert," I began.

"Jesus, I know that," George said, a little too abruptly for my taste. I have been interested in photography for quite a while, and although I'm certainly an amateur, I do know a few things about the subject. George's rudeness surprised me, for usually he's the model of inoffensiveness. I've been his best friend for years, almost the only one in town he can talk to, and even with me he can talk of nothing but photography. He lives with his superannuated mother, which is probably part of his problem. I've always felt sorry for him.

"I'm no expert," I repeated, "but these are really good. Almost brilliant, I'd say. Detail, contrast, composition. . . ."

"Sure," George broke in, not at all satisfied. "But did you notice anything else?"

"Keep your trousers on, George," I said. He slumped down in the booth, his long, bird-thin chest seeming sunken and his adenoidal face twitching slightly. "It's some trick of the light or the perspective or something, isn't it?" I picked up the top print. "This one, for instance. At first I didn't even recognize the scene, I thought it must be some old, well-kept farm-house in Pennsylvania or maybe the west of England, don't ask me why. But these were taken right outside town, weren't they? It's the Rayne place, isn't it?"

George nodded and waited for me to continue. I was appar-ently getting to what he was interested in. "You've somehow managed to make everything seem more solid, better cared for, just, well, prettier, richer, but more than that. Here. The freeway cuts close there, but here you can't even tell it's there. That stand of trees gives the impression of being part of a forest. The barn looks white-washed clean as the snow banks around it; I've driven past the place for thirty years, and I don't think it's seen a brush in all that time. Other things I can't put my finger on. You should go into advertising, George. I mean it," sliding the envelope toward him.

"They're not mine," George said. "I just finished develop-ing them for a customer. Arne Jansen."

I snorted. Arne Jansen is a failed farmer who rents the Rayne place and now works almost full time at the feed store to make a living. The farm is practically worthless, now, though once it did well.

"Arne Jansen," I said, "didn't take these pictures. He wouldn't know which way to point a camera and would make a balls of it if somebody showed him." I've gotten to know Arne at town meetings. He's nice enough, I suppose, but dull as dirt. I once had to explain what a microfilm reader was to him three times before he would agree to vote on one.

"He didn't know anything about cameras, you're right," George said, "and he may still not. But he took these pictures. I sold him the camera, three weeks ago. I've no idea how the notion got into his head. Maybe some picture book gave him the idea, I don't know."

I recalled that Arne did look at magazines from time to time. He comes into the library sometimes when he's waiting for his wife to pick him up from work. Sometimes he goes over and looks at the microfilm reader, but mostly he flips through magazines, never saying anything. For a while I thought he had a crush on Gloria, but he's never said a word to her. Little good it would have done him. She's got her mind on bigger fish than us. You can't keep a man from thinking, though, that's what I always say.

I said, "If Arne Jansen took these pictures, then you must have sold him some fancy computerized camera that he'll be the rest of his life paying off on, and you should be ashamed. But I still think you're pulling my leg."

"Jesus Christ, would you shut up and listen!" George shouted then, half-rising over the table. For a second it occurred to me that he was going to hit me, incredible as it seems, but I was too amazed to move. The place was packed; everyone stared at us. Marie hurried out from behind the counter to see what was going on. When she saw it was George, hunched over the table of the booth like a great bulge-eyed crane, she stopped short, as surprised as the rest of us. George is the most serious, quiet man in town, and it's a quiet town.

"Everything all right here?" Marie asked. Seeming suddenly to realize his position, George sank back with an embarrassed groan.

"Sure, Marie," I said. "George here just got a little excited. It was bound to happen one of these years. Now he'll be good for another forty years." That got some chuckles from the nearby tables.

Unamused, Marie looked at George, then at me, then returned to the grill.

"Sorry," George mumbled, "I don't know. . . . I know this is pretty odd, believe me." He sat beating his knuckles rhythmically against his bowed, bony forehead.

With anyone but George I would have gotten up and left about this time. I'm not a psychiatrist, and crazy people make me nervous. But, as I said, I was his best friend, and usually he

was the image of steadiness, kind to his old mother, certainly
not a joker.

"Go on, George," I said, "finish the story. I won't interrupt
again, I promise."

"Maybe I should just shut up about this whole thing," he
said, still staring down and striking his forehead, though more
slowly. "But I thought I could trust you. I have to talk to
somebody."

"Of course you can trust me, George, just keep your voice
down. And stop rapping on your forehead."

He folded his hands in front of him and took a deep breath.
"All right," he said, "all right." He seemed almost normal. I
had hopes, then, of finishing my lunch.

"When Arne asked for a camera," George said, "I assumed
he meant something inexpensive like an Instamatic, and that's
what I showed him. He only glanced at it. 'That's a toy,' he
said, 'I want a real camera,' and pointed to a big Pentax SLR.
Well, I almost smiled at this — you know what a penny-
pincher he usually is, and what a time he has making ends
meet. But I've seen it before, somebody sees a photograph
that hits him in a way that he has to start taking pictures, too.
Or looks at photography magazines for the nudes, and somehow gets hooked on the process itself. All kinds of people,
you'd be surprised. They always go in full barrel, and usually
they lose interest once they discover there's a trick to getting
the kind of picture they had in mind."

I was able to finish my macaroni and cheese special while
George was telling me this, though it had gotten pretty rubbery by then. I motioned to Marie for a couple coffees. She set
them down before us, clearly relieved that George had settled
down. When those quiet ones act up it's pretty upsetting.
George may never have seen the cup; it sat there going cold
while he cracked his big knuckles.

George went on. "'Well, that's a real camera, all right,
Arne,' I told him, 'but it's four-fifty, list. I couldn't give it to
you for less than three-seventy-five.' I said it as gentle as I

could, but his face fell. I thought a minute, then remembered an old thirty-five millimeter rangefinder I've had around the shop for years, don't even know where it came from. Has a broken light meter, but everything else seemed to be in good shape. I let him have it cheap, and he took it. I tried to explain how to operate it, but he was really coming in cold, so it took a long time before he even began to catch on about focus and exposure.

"He paid me cash, and I threw in a few rolls of film. You hate to take advantage of a guy like that."

This was all interesting, but it hardly seemed worth the agitation George had displayed earlier. It was getting past my lunch hour. I try to be back at the library by one-thirty, though pretty, little Gloria is able to run the place quite well without me, and she brings her lunch and eats it behind the circulation desk. So I didn't interrupt him. I guess I did glance at my watch.

"All right," George said, "I'm getting to it. In a week or so Arne's wife drops off a roll of film to be developed. Mainly wanted the excuse to come in and let me know what she thought of me for selling Arne that camera and getting him started on all that foolishness, I think. She's a hard case. Anyway, those are the prints," he concluded, gesturing toward the envelope in front of me.

"Look, George," I said, "don't take offense, but you know as well — better — than I that a beginner doesn't take pictures like these, not with an old rangefinder, with or without a lightmeter. One or two out of twenty, maybe, by accident, but not a whole roll. Forgetting the tricky perspectives and so forth. Not one is out of focus, the detail is incredible, depth of field, focus, everything. What are you up to?"

"Those are Arne's pictures," George said, "and I did nothing but develop them." I looked at him a moment, and then shrugged. He was telling the truth. The flat tone of his voice convinced me where my reason refused. I realized that it was just this contradiction between what he knew about photography and what he had seen that was upsetting him. He's so damn serious about everything, such a sensitive plant; I think it comes from living with his mother all these years. It's not natural.

"Well, then, George," I said, "the man must simply be a freak. This is his genius. Or else it's just dumb luck. Look, when he learns something he'll start screwing up like the rest of us." George gave a mirthless smile, but shook his head. He had the most miserable look on his face.

"You haven't seen them all," he said, in a voice that was practically a groan.

By now I was getting a bit tired of the game and said nothing. Since George had been my friend for years, I owed him some patience, but this was getting to be a little much.

After a second he drew another envelope out of his inner coat pocket, and after a moment's hesitation, laid it before me. I didn't wait to be told to open it, and almost laughed when I discovered it was sealed. But then I noticed the expression on George's face, which would have sobered a loon.

I opened the envelope with a table knife; there were two prints inside, with the same glitteringly clear focus and fine detail as the others. The first was a picture of Arne's wife, a tall, hatchet-faced woman standing before the barn, her dark, gaunt figure standing on a snowy path beneath the glinting, ragged points of the ice mass that hung far down from the eaves. She stood there with obvious annoyance, caught in the middle of her chores, judging from her dress, caught against the stark white barn.

It was an effective picture, but I was a little surprised to see that Arne's apparent gift for finding the angle and light that made everything look better hadn't improved the image of his wife, which surely needed improvement.

I turned to the second picture then, took one look, and then understood why George was upset. I set both prints down shakily and had to swallow carefully a few times. The ice had given way, apparently an instant before the shutter snapped.

The photograph showed the woman crushed and impaled by the mass of yard-long icicles, some as thick at the top as a man's thigh. Some stood upright still, pierced through her body into the frozen ground.

George looked at me with his earlier wild look clamped rigidly into impassivity. Then I remembered something. "Didn't you say that she. . . ." I gestured at the photograph.

"That's right," he said. "She brought them in to be developed."

"It's a trick, then."

"Not a chance," George said. "He doesn't, couldn't know enough to do that," he tapped the print, "so convincingly."

"Well, what do you think, then?" I asked.

"What do *you* think?"

I looked at him. He was the last person in the world to consider a practical joke, and that eliminated the one possibility that was at all rational. I shrugged. "Wish fulfillment?"

He nodded. "Nothing else explains it: the perfect negatives, transformed scenes, and that." I followed his eyes to the print. "It's impossible, of course, but there you are." He seemed a bit less oppressed, now that I shared his peculiar knowledge, if knowledge is the word for it. He leaned back, cracking his knuckles, his flat cheeks twitching almost invisibly.

"What are you going to do?" I asked him. It's surprising how easy it is to accept the impossible when there's no alternative. "What are you going to do, George?"

"I don't know," he said, still looking pale, but better than before. "Destroy these, I guess, first. All of them, and say there was something wrong with the camera. Then try to get the camera back."

"You're sure it's the camera, not him?"

He hadn't considered the possibility, but there was certainly no reason to be sure about anything at that point. Only by letting Arne shoot a roll with another camera, we agreed, could we know that the impossibility George had discovered didn't originate in some odd quality of Arne himself, and that the camera made no difference.

As it turned out, after all the hell he'd been catching from his wife (the attempted flattery of photographing her had not succeeded), Arne was only too happy to sell the camera back. But he wanted nothing but his money in exchange. He was through with photography, he told George. He wasn't sure what he'd ever seen in it, anyway.

I dropped into George's shop a few days later to see how his experiments were coming with what we were by then calling the wish-fulfillment camera. He wasn't out front, so I went back to see if he was in the darkroom.

He was. The warning light was on, so I knocked to let him know I was there, then settled down with one of his photography magazines, remembering a time when those were hot stuff for me. I was in no hurry. Nobody much comes into the library that time of day. Besides, Gloria had been more than usually chilly towards me recently, so there would have been nothing with which to occupy myself.

After a while I knocked again and shouted in to him, asking how long he would be in there. There was no reply. I tried the door and found it was locked. But the latch gave in to a bit of bullying.

I saw him crumpled in the corner even before I switched on the light. He was snoring irregularly, his hand resting defensively on a partially emptied six-pack. I thought, What kind of man passes out on four beers? Knows it would be enough? That was George. Already I suspected what had happened. Before I left, embarrassed, I noticed the open camera and the film that was still smoldering in a pan of acid. He hadn't gotten all of it in the pan — that suggests that he started getting drunk (pathetic drunk!) before destroying, perhaps before developing, the negatives.

With a pair of tweezers I fished out the one partially intact frame and held it up to the light. Then I slipped it back into the acid. It was a picture of George's mother. He should have known better than that, even somebody as naive as George. Well, live and learn, I always say.

I took the camera with me when I left, assuming, correctly, I think, that George would rather not have to face it when he came around. I've seen him since then, but we haven't had a chance to speak. I'll have to mention it to him, to let him know the camera is in safe hands.

Yes, I've been doing my own little experiments. Why don't you drop by the library some day, after hours? I'll show you some things that I think you'll find amusing. You've met Gloria, haven't you? Ah.

HE LIVED ALONE, AND WHEN
there was no one with him he
kept the radio on continuously. In
principle he did not approve of
using music as a background for
other things. But it was an old
habit and he did it without thinking.

Background Music

On this occasion he had quit
working an hour or so after mid-
night. After he had undressed and turned out the lights he
stood a moment beside the radio. A violin concerto was being
broadcast. In a different mood he would have lain down on
the covers in the darkness and listened the piece through to its
end before turning it off.

But things had not been going well for him. He was de-
pressed and it did not seem he would solve the problem soon.
And so, in a gesture like the pointless crushing of a beautiful
insect, in the middle of a rising scale he abruptly switched the
radio off and went to bed. He lay restlessly for a time before
falling into a sullen, dreamless sleep.

After the radio had been turned off, the unheard, unresolved
sound of the violin kept rising, climbing by itself steadily
past the upper limit of human hearing. All over that part of
town for a moment dogs barked in their sleep, and the late
prowlers among garbage cans stretched their throats taut and
howled up in perplexity, knowing that something awful was
happening.

But that was over almost before the forlorn wailings from
dark alleyways had time to flow darkly together. And the
violin's sound rose into the region of little crystals and the fine
edges of surgical knives. The distances are enormous there,
and each new dimension of pitch takes longer to reach.

It was almost four, when he was almost inanimate in the pit
of deepest sleep, that an unthinkable white light burst un-
thinkably, suddenly, in his head, enveloping the sluggish
synapse in mid-flight, leaving the records of coffee taste and
faces and difficult conversations floating for an instant, mind-

less, lost in the suddenly empty, immense room of his skull, before vanishing too, like the warm breath in a child's exploded balloon.

The Labors of Love

ED ROCKED GENTLY IN THE OLD chair, his gaze focused on the arched refrigerator humming in the corner of his efficiency apartment. He concentrated on its motor, drawing the ammonia gas into the pump, compressing it, driving off the nervous load of heat, sending the suddenly frigid gas pulsing through the maze of copper tubes gathering frost above some frozen, frost-encrusted beans. The chair creaked — a Japanese Boston rocker — and without completely dropping the refrigerator from his thoughts he concentrated on the chair's glued joints around and under him, pulling moisture into the parched glue, swelling the shrunken dowels. Gradually the cheap, turned wood knit itself more tightly together.

He shifted, and found that the squeaking had stopped. In the next apartment, Mrs. Garvey flushed her toilet, and he willed the cold water from the tank to rush out, washing away her small, hard turds. Then, drawing the corroded brass bulb to the bottom of the tank, he sprang the valve which drew the plunger which released fresh water to fill the tank again. The pipes trembled and groaned and finally shuddered to a stop as the float was lifted to the top of the tank, closing the intake valve. He relaxed a little, then, his mind touching lightly, floating across each of the room's few objects.

Besides the rocker, the only furniture was a home-made platform bed, low to the floor, with massive four-by-four legs. Underneath the one-inch plywood platform was a framework of cross-ribs and a center spine, a sort of keel stabilizing the flat, blunt boat. For a mattress there was a pad of old army blankets folded and sewn together with heavy, waxed, shoemaker's twine. It was summer, and the only bedclothes consisted of a large sheet, doubled over lengthwise and sewn with the same twine into a gigantic pillowcase. There was no pillow. Bolted to one wall was an old oak bookcase filled with the massive volumes of an eleventh

Britannica, an encyclopedia of home repairs, Gray's Anatomy, auto repair manuals, an atlas, almanacs, textbooks on nuclear and astro physics, architecture, botany, chemistry, zoology. Everything was in order: the togglebolts securing the bookcase to the wall were tight, the bindings of the books were holding up, the stitching in the blanket-mattress was secure, double-knotted. The bed itself was strong as stone: pegged, glued, screwed together into unbudging solidity. His mind rested on it gratefully.

It was a weekday morning in late June; sun poured into the room and the abundant, random dust rushed up to meet it, warm and delirious with pleasure. Ed kept the whole room of them from colliding for a moment, purely as an exercise, then rose, pulled on his high-topped, steel-toed work boots, laced and knotted them, knotted them again, then left his apartment and climbed steadily down the seven flights of narrow, dangerous stairs to the green-tiled lobby. Stepping outside, he blinked in the sun, closed the apartment house door firmly behind him, checking to see that the latch had caught. From the last of the worn stone steps he headed uptown, his arms and legs swinging in deliberate, perfect, and rather stiff alternation. He walked with his eyes straight ahead, yet noting everything around him, pushing back the leaning tenements, encouraging the hopeless saplings parked four to a block, which would not be saved from savagery by the iron posts and twisted wires that held them upright.

Suddenly he stopped; an old, arthritic dog was crossing the street towards him, limping stiffly, its body hunched and contracted until its rear legs nearly touched the front. He concentrated carefully on the dog's awkward movements, carefully lifting one foot at a time, carefully setting it down: front left, rear right, front right, rear left. There were no cars at the moment, only one sanitation truck approaching, still a block away.

And then he heard a woman's voice calling to him from high above the street. "Eddy! Eddy, hey!" He turned, looked up, shading his eyes against the late morning sun. "Eddy, come up here, you bastard!" the voice cried again, and the old dog, suddenly helpless, trying to take two steps at the same time, stumbled, fell in a heap, still yards from the curb. Ed turned back, saw what had happened; the big truck roared toward the pile of white and brown fur, swerved away at the last moment, sailed over the curb, mashed explosively into a row of garbage cans, and drove halfway through the stairway of a brownstone duplex. After a moment, the door of the smashed truck swung open and the driver climbed slowly out, followed by his partner. They stood on the sidewalk in their overalls and heavy gloves, staring in awe at the devastation. The driver shook his head slowly. "What kind of joker would roll a baby buggy into the street, huh?" His partner nodded dully, then turned and looked at him strangely. "What?" he asked. "What baby buggy? I didn't see nothing but that crazy Volkswagen."

Ed helped the dog the rest of the way across the street and then entered the building from which the voice had called to him. He climbed the dark stairs to a fourth-floor apartment, knocked, waited a moment, then walked in. A woman was leaning out the window, who said when he entered, "What a mess," her head and shoulders a good ways out the window. "Thank God I was watching."

"I feel bad about the truck," Ed said to her bent back, "they're very expensive."

"Those guys seem to be O.K.," she marveled, leaning still farther out the window, the thin seat of her faded jeans stretched smooth. "Look at them down there," she said, "standing around like they don't know what happened." Then she said, "Let go of me, you mother!" He let go of her. "Sally," he said. "Shut up, you son of a bitch crazy asshole," she said. "You incredible damn prick."

He stood in the center of her airy, high-ceilinged apartment, resting gently on the balls of his feet, arms crossed, listening to the tiny tapping in his inner ears, feeling the blood sail through his arteries and veins, at the same time feeling himself drawn into the similar and different rhythms of the woman's body, tense and furious before him. He had not eaten for several days, and his stomach was a small, serene knot in the center of his body. She stood in front of him, as tall as he was, cursing him, as he silently said the words along with her, his tongue curling and dancing in the closed cage of his teeth, articulating every syllable, his breath moving in his throat with her breath.

Finally she collapsed in a heap on the bare wood floor, crying and gasping, hiccuping and furious. He sat on the floor beside her, cross-legged, patting her on the back to help her breathe more easily until she could speak again. Gradually her breath matched itself to his own calm breath.

"You said you were coming with me to my sister's wedding," she moaned, "and then when I try to call you up, they've disconnected your phone, you jerk," she said, "how could you let them do it? And then I get worried and come over and you creep, nobody answers the door, you unbelievable bastard," she cried, "how can you say you love me and then let them disconnect your phone, and then I see you goddamn strolling by," she screamed and threw herself at him beating at his head and chest with her fists, her thumbs grasped by her furiously clamped fingers.

"Careful," he said to her, holding her wrists, prying open her fingers to release the thumbs. "You'll break them one of these days," he said. "I've told you about that." He spoke very softly, continuing to hold her.

"How can you say you love me?" she moaned, relaxing in his grip, going limp on the floor.

"I love you," he said. "I love everything." She burst into tears again; he helped her to her feet and led her to the bed. She lay down obediently, sobbing erratically, burying her face and fists in the pillow. He sat on the edge of the bed, gently stroking her back, relaxing the tense muscles in her neck and shoulders.

"I feel bad about the wedding," he said after a time. "Oh, hell," she groaned, rolling over, almost smiling through her tear-distorted face. "It didn't come off anyway," she said. "They had the hall rented, tuxes, dresses, the works, it was going to be a big deal. Then an old girlfriend of his comes over the night before and tells her something about him, I don't know what, and she called it all off."

"I feel bad about that," he said. He sat holding her hands, she was forgiving him, and he was conscious of the pulse in her fingers, of the great weight of the building pressing itself steadfastly against the earth, of smoke rising from an incinerator faithfully into the clouds. After a while he went into her kitchen and scrambled some eggs, which they ate together, and then he left and walked down to the Number Nine tavern.

Ed stepped inside, blinded a moment in the dim, pleasant shadows of a tavern in the middle of the day. He looked around, nodded to the regulars slouched along the long bar, joined them, and ordered a beer. As he pressed the countless bubbles against the smooth, unyielding walls of the stainless steel tank below the bar, forcing up the foaming stream of alcohol into the tapering spigot, he watched the men at the bar. One of them, with a polka-dotted cloth hat pulled low over his forehead, was Mrs. Garvey's son, who almost never visited her. He was having a few drinks to gather courage before having lunch with her. The old man at the end of the bar was once an important city politician. His dreams, as he sat on the worn stool, were violently and purely political. He was extremely happy, and rarely felt the need to talk to anyone. The one newcomer at the bar was a very lonely young man, just in from L.A., unemployed, who had never before taken a drink before noon. He would have a good job by the end of the week, and by fall he would be courting, successfully, Sally's sister. Ed smiled a secret smile at him, toasted him with the drink he was about to receive.

"Nice day, Ed," the bartender said, sliding the foaming

glass toward him. "Thanks, John," he said. The beer was golden, filled with all the goodness of the morning. He sipped quietly at the rich head, while the bartender, sleepy still, leaned against the bar, his big forearms crossed on the polished mahogany.

"John?"

"Hmm?" the bartender answered.

"John, love makes the world go round."

"You bet it does," the bartender said, grinning sleepily.

Ed drew off the last of the foam, felt the cold beer wash his mouth, his tongue turning precious. He was conscious of the mug melting patiently between his hands, the bottle-fronted mirror forming his reflection to the best of its ability, the softly polished wood of the bar cradling his elbows. "It does," he said to the big, sleepy man. "It really does."

A Very Short Story

A MAN IS AT A PARTY WITH HIS former lover and her new husband. She is in one part of the room with her husband, talking with some old friends. He is a little ways off, telling a story. And then he starts making a peculiar kittenish, rhythmical crying sound, then continues with his story.

She and her husband do not look at each other. It is the sound she makes while making love. He does not pay any attention to them. The story is not about her; it is just that the woman in his story makes the same sound in bed as she makes. There is a certain tension in the room.

A Nest of Hooks

"I'M NOT SURE I LIKE THIS stereotyped division of labor," she says. He is sitting on the tarp before their tent, his fishing gear spread out before him. He is trying to get everything back in order in his tackle box, while she packs up their cooking utensils and the remaining food.

"Yeah," he says, "you're right, I hadn't thought about it. Well, here." He stands. "You finish this up, I'll finish the kitchen stuff."

"Really?" she says. "You're beautiful." As he starts stuffing plastic bags of flour and oatmeal into their wooden camp kitchen, she crouches in front of his tackle box and the nest of hooks and baits spread out on the tarp. "What were you doing?" she asks.

"Just try to untangle that mess of plugs and put each one in a compartment," he says. "Then sort of arrange the rest of the stuff in the bottom of the box." The box had spilled in the boat the night before, and in the dark he had simply tossed everything back in.

She carefully begins to separate the lures from each other, linked together in complicated ways by their treble hooks. She has never before looked at his collection of plugs very carefully. When she fishes, she prefers to stick with one, maybe two lures that appeal to her. He has admitted that usually the particular lure probably doesn't make too much difference, but still he is changing them all the time. She favors a weedless copper spoon, to which she attaches a strip of white pork rind.

She has the kit pretty well organized when she notices a lure she has not seen before. It is a little silver minnow of highly polished plastic, about the length and thickness of her little finger. It is jointed in the middle and has the usual two sets of treble hooks. Something about it holds her attention; it is like a little jewel, so fine and graceful is it, with beautiful little amber eyes bulging from its delicate head, a drop of black shining in their depths. Infinitely fine, tiny scales are etched on its tapering, almost translucent sides. Though she can see the hardware — the metal lip, the eyelet, the joint, the hanging hooks — it is incredibly lifelike.

"How's it going?" he asks her after closing the lid of the kitchen box. She starts back from him, stumbles back against the tent, catches herself, backs away from him, her eyes fixed on him as she stumbles backward, one hand clenched before her mouth.

"What's the matter?" he shouts. "What's going on?"

What Happened to Bill Day?

"PHILIP," I SAY, "YOU LITTLE bourgeois fake."

"What?" he says, "what?" lifting his curly, bull-calf head, the muscles of his forearm tensing as he grips the thin pedal wrench. "What?"

"Get back to work, Philip," I say. He squints at me down the shop's single, crowded aisle, grinning at me uncertainly. "Kulak," I say.

He shakes his head at me, laughs, begins to fasten a pedal to the child's bicycle he is assembling in the back of the shop. I watch him from a stool in front, beside the dysfunctional cash register. "You're nothing like Bill Day, that's for sure," he says.

"What happened to Bill Day?" I ask. Bill Day, his absence, is the reason why I am sitting beside this wrecked cash register, high on this wooden stool, selling bicycles. But for Bill Day, his missing person, I would still be working as a mechanic in back of the big store on Houston Street, north of the Village. Because of him, his disappearance, I no longer set up bicycles and fix flats in the huge and shabby old bicycle warehouse downtown. But for him, I would be a part of that Babel still, still working with the two old Italians who build wheels and frames and sing out together in high, operatic tenors; with Puerto Rican Jesús, who speaks nothing but Spanish and does most of the heavy lifting; with Mohammed Mohammed, cock-vain bicycle road racer; and with a crowd of West Indians speaking their sweet music of confusion: from Albert Fox, as much Brooklyn in his tongue, now, as Barbados, to Johnson, a slow, slow old man who sweeps up; Johnson, who speaks a Jamaican patois of such dark, heavy richness that, for all of me, he might be speaking Turkish. President Johnson, we called him. Because of what happened to Bill Day (what happened?) I am no longer working down there under the eyes of the Rogetti brothers, manic Milanese who have builded a bicycle empire in Little Italy. I am stationed here instead, in one of their uptown colonies, manager of this two-man outpost in the east seventies.

No one knows what happened to Bill Day. Nick came back one day, told me to stop what I was doing, change my clothes, take the Second Avenue bus uptown. He gave me the keys, twenty bucks for the register, explained the burglar alarm system, how to turn it off, said it was a great opportunity for me, he would be up that evening. "What happened to Bill Day?" I asked him. He didn't know.

"Philip," I say, "I'm going downstairs to check the stock. Mind the store, don't nationalize, please."

"You bet," he says. He drops his tools, saunters up to the front, settles down on the chair behind the counter. He rummages underneath for one of a stack of skin magazines stored there, magazines of women with mammoth breasts. These magazines are the legacy of Bill Day.

"The American Dream," Philip marvels, "a chick with tits so big she can touch her earlobes with her nipples." He is still in high school, a very intelligent kid, a revolutionary.

I go out in front of the shop, unpadlock the heavy iron doors set in the sidewalk, lift them with difficulty and prop them open, hoping nobody drops through, and climb down the dark steps into the cellar below the store. I make as much noise as possible, alerting the rats. I don't like it down here, it is dark and filthy, junk piled about hopelessly, and I don't need to check the stock, really; I have a record upstairs of all the cartoned bikes stored down here. I walk down the rows of flat boxes, dimly lighted by a single bulb, checking their coded contents against my list. I pull a few to bring up for display. In the corners and on several long tables there are dusty stacks of white work shirts, all smalls, with extremely narrow collars — relics of a day when the shop was a laundry. I push a stack over, the spilled shirts glow white where dirt has not settled. There is no trace of Bill Day, no explanation.

"I came to work one day," Philip tells me, "and the shop was locked. I sat down on the curb and read awhile, then went down to the karate school. I was working just Tuesdays and Thursdays then; same thing happened on Thursday, so I called downtown. Nick was sore as hell, said he'd look into it. Saturday I came down and worked with you guys. Next thing, they have you up here, and it's regular as prunes again."

"What was he like?" I ask him, "Bill Day."

"Nothing special," he says. "Not too smart. Not a mechanic, either; I had to do all the repair work. He just tried to sell bikes. He wanted to sell hundreds of bikes."

"You're still supposed to do the repairs," I say.

"Sure," Philip laughs, "but you like to take a part. You feel guilty about being a boss."

"Philip," I say. He laughs.

From Danny, the driver who brings me bikes and parts from downtown, I learn that Bill's mother had notified the police when he didn't show up at home for two days. A missing persons is out for him, nobody has a clue.

"You want to know what I think?" he asks, Danny, a city-stunted, skinny guy in filthy sleeveless undershirt, cunning rat's face always unshaven. "Know what I fucking think?" he asks. I wait for him to tell me. "I think he was fucking hit."

"Hit?" I say. "Bill Day?"

"Hit," he says, "fucking right. You want to know why?" I wait for him to tell me. "Because he fucking knew too much."

"I'll help you unload these bikes, Danny," I say, jumping into the van, pushing the boxes toward the tailgate.

"You don't know about Nick's connections with the mob?" Danny holds the door open for me as I carry a bike into the store, then follows after me as I go to grab another. "You think they make all their fucking money selling bicycles? Fixing flat fucking tires?"

"Danny," I say, pulling bikes off the truck, stacking them on the sidewalk, "the Rogetti's are bastards, but they're in that goddamn store twelve hours a day, six, seven days a week. You're full of shit, the mob."

"He was wasted," Danny insists, "you don't know shit." After we have unloaded the van he goes into the deli next door and comes back with a beer. He sits down on my stool, stares out the door at two young women, office girls, probably, who are walking by. "Didn't I tell you?" he asks. "Ain't this the fucking greatest place? More good-looking broads here than anyplace in the city. In the world. Am I right or wrong?" It is one of Nick Rogetti's stock expressions, "Am I right or wrong?"

"It's O.K.," I tell him.

He spits on the floor. "Fucking clown. I'd give my ass to work up here. The guys downtown, they try to pay me to let them make deliveries up here, I tell them to go to hell."

"You're married, Danny," I say, "you have a wife and kid."

His voice becomes softer, though his eyes continue to rake the street. "Sure," he says. "You know what my life is fucking like? I got two jobs: drive truck and work in the warehouse during the day, load trailers on the west side in the evening. I get home nine, ten o'clock, too tired to eat. I don't even get laid. Sometimes I get laid," he says, "but usually I'm fucking dead."

"It's tough," I say. He's so small.

"Fucking right it's tough," he says. He zings the empty can out the door at a passing bus, grabs his invoice sheet, goes out to his truck, jumps in. "See you, kid," he says.

"See you, Danny."

When Philip comes in to work that afternoon, I tell him what Danny said happened to Bill Day. He surprises me by taking it with a straight face. "It's not just the mob, though," he says. "The C.I.A. was behind it. And they weren't really after Bill." I know what he is going to say, it's his main theme, his persecution by the C.I.A. The C.I.A. and F.B.I. are

on him all the time. Disguised as meter readers for this building they descend into the cellar under the shop to check the
taps they have on him.

"Why you, Phil?" I ask, as I have asked before. "Because
you've seen *The Battle of Algiers* fourteen times? Because
you're learning to kill with your bare hands? Because you
wear fatigues?"

"I don't wear fatigues!" he shouts, and I laugh. I know this
gets him. "Those goddamn fakes," he says, "that's the way to
spot a pseudo-revolutionary, see if he's wearing army surplus.
Goddamn combat boots, for God's sake." Philip is very serious about the revolution, and I have to be careful how hard I
push him on the subject. He is about sixteen, trying to grow a
beard. When he talks about the revolution, he is hard and
dangerous.

"Philip," I say, "I've been thinking about all those shirts in
the cellar."

"Yeah?" he says, still wary. He can't stand it sometimes
when I joke about the revolution. He could kill me with a
single blow upon the breastbone, he has told me, and I believe him.

"I'm tired of selling bicycles, Philip," I say. "I think it's
time we turned this place back into a laundry."

"Oh yeah!" he says, on my side again, "oh yeah! Mike and
Nick will come up to see what the hell's this they heard."

"And there we'll be," I say, "you and I in white coats,
standing behind the counter between piles of linen."

"No tickee, no takee," Philip says, "solly Nick."

"It will kill him, Phil," I say. "It will stop his wop heart."

"You know," Philip says, "I've always loved the smell of
laundries. I mean, it's beautiful, isn't it?"

"It is," I say, "it's the steam and the soap. That clean, wet,
warm smell, there's nothing like it, Phil. Am I right or
wrong?" We go on like this a good part of the day, while
customers wait to be sold ten-speed bicycles. A man in a
beautiful linen suit interrupts us; he's going to spend three or

four hundred dollars. Philip goes back to work on some set-ups. It's a pretty good day.

If Danny is perhaps wrong about what happened to Bill Day, he is right about the girls in this neighborhood. About three in the afternoon a woman comes in to buy a bicycle. She is about thirty; dark, fine-boned, beautiful face, built like an angel, and she is wearing a jump suit of see-through black lace. No panties, no bra. An embroidered design of some kind keeps you from seeing pussy, but that's about it. Before I know it, Philip is up front with me, jabbering to her about ten-speeds and three-speeds, giving her a line of double-talk. "Better finish those set-ups, Phil," I say to him, "I can handle it up here." He shows her the dynohub on a deluxe Raleigh, spinning the front wheel to make it work. He doesn't notice that it isn't hooked up.

"Excuse me," I say to her, and she smiles at me. I take Philip by the arm, draw him toward the back of the shop. It is not easy to make it seem casual, for he is quite strong, though short. "I want to show you something, Philip," I say, and push him out the back door of the shop into the little asphalt courtyard there, the bottom of an airshaft. He steps back to catch his balance, I slam the door, lock it, and return to the front of the store, smiling apologetically. She laughs, I laugh with her. The door is very heavy, a fire door, and Philip's pounding is sufficiently muffled for me to complete the transaction with a certain degree of aplomb.

"Philip," I say later, letting him in again, "I'm sorry, it was for your own good."

"I know it," he says.

"Even I, Phil, the boss, almost fainted when she tried one out for size."

"I believe it," he says.

"Philip," I say, "if you had seen her straddling that bike, bending over the bars, it would have driven you out of your young mind."

"I know it," he says, sitting down on an empty bike carton.

"I couldn't help myself. Thank you for saving me from my still untamed natural instincts."

"Here," I say, "go next door to the deli and buy yourself a soda. Get me a Vernors, please." When he is gone, I ask him, "What happened to Bill Day? Was he lost in big tits? Did he die of love?"

When Philip returns with his coke and my ginger ale, I tell him about a Puerto Rican kid who was in the deli the other day, bragging about his skill in baseball and basketball. "I'm good at all sports," he told the old man behind the counter, making sandwiches. The old man winked at me and asked the kid, "How are you at pocket pool?" "I'm good at all sports," the kid insisted again, and the old man almost choked to death laughing.

Philip chuckles, and then asks me if I'd ever noticed that the butt of all my stories are ethnics, usually Puerto Ricans. I say they are not, but that, after all, what else is there in this town?

"It's really a class thing," he says, "you feel contempt for the poor."

"Who?" I ask, "who are the poor? I make less than three thousand dollars a year. I don't have a television, a car, a stereo. I don't have a suit."

"For now," he says, "for now you don't. You're a student, an intellectual, an elitist."

"My old man never made more than eight thousand dollars a year," I say. "How much does your father make, Phil? Forty? Fifty grand?"

"I can't help that," he says. "That has nothing to do with me."

"Where do you live, Phil? Who paid for your Frejus?"

"Red herrings!" he laughs. "You always do that." It's true, I always do. I don't care a damn about politics, really, or economics. What I want to know is, what happened to Bill Day?

Philip comes to me one day and asks me to order a bunch of very expensive Campagnola parts from downtown: crank set, seatpost, dérailleurs, brakes. "Why?" I ask him. No customer has asked for them.

"I'm going to upgrade my Frejus," he says.

"They'll cost a mint," I say, "even with your discount."

"I thought I'd take a *real* discount," he says. "You don't mind, do you?"

"I don't mind," I say, "but I won't let you."

"Why not?" he grins, "why so pious? They're crooked themselves, they expect you to rip them off a little." It's true, they cut every corner they can, more for the art of it than for the money, I believe. The Rogetti brothers have a passion for deviousness. Instead of giving me the raise I asked for, they pay my overtime out of unrecorded rentals, saving me on taxes. When I worked downtown, they were always taking me aside, promising me a great future in their organization, telling me not to tell the other mechanics how much they were paying me. They have ordered me never to admit the connection between this shop and the main store downtown; they refuse to talk to anyone on the telephone.

"You're going to have to pay for your damn parts, Phil," I say.

"You know what your hangup is?" he asks. "Private property. You're an intellectual, but you worship private property. Private property *is* crime," he says, "so how can it be a crime to steal it?" He is enjoying this, he doesn't really care about the parts.

"Philip," I say, "you talk like Marcuse, but your heart is the heart of a Rockefeller. Possessions are so important to you, you'd risk your freedom. That's the real *crime* of crime," I say, "the risk of your freedom." We argue on and on, having a pretty good time, until Philip has to leave for his karate lesson.

He is right about me, I am pathetically, pathologically honest. I have nightmares of imprisonment, execution, and I always know that I have it coming. Downtown they must think I'm working some new racket, I send along so much profit. I wonder, is this what happened to Bill Day? Was he guilty? No money was missing. So what happened?

When Philip is gone I get a lot of work done, setting up bicycles, doing repairs. I hate to work much while he's around, it's so bourgeois, except for doing the more interesting jobs. He and I were up front, once, talking. I am repairing a tubular tire, an intricate job, while he watches. I have the thin natural rubber tube pulled out a little from the incision, like a fine, pink intestine, when this dwarf comes in to look for a bike for his "lady friend," he says. He looks at some full-sized adult models, then comes over and watches me. Suddenly he roars with laughter, whips a condom out of his pocket, loose, like a balloon, not rolled up in a wrapper, and asks me if I could patch *that* for him. Philip laughs like hell, I am too startled. The dwarf doesn't buy anything.

When he is gone, I tell Philip about a guy I used to know in school, a guy named Steve Shattuck, from Nutley, New Jersey, who used to make obscene answers on the telephone. Someone would call, and it would be a wrong number. The guy would say, "Is Gene there?" or something, and Shattuck would answer, "Eat me raw, cocksucker," and so forth, until the caller would hang up.

"Whatever happened to him?" Philip asks. "Did he ever get caught?"

"How could he get caught?" I ask. "It was the other guy's fault, he should have been more careful." Philip tilts back his head and howls appreciatively. Except when he is talking about the revolution, Philip is just like any other kid. I know he is going to try a Shattuck the next time he gets a wrong number. "Nothing ever happened to Steve Shattuck," I say.

At night I am alone in the shop. When the park is open late, I keep the shop open till nine or so, sitting behind the counter, renting a few bikes, doing the books. It's pretty quiet, usually. Old men walk by alone; they stop, look at the bikes in the display window. After a while they come in, and seeing that I'm not busy, they ask me about the bicycles or something. "I see you carry some Italian bikes," one says. "Do the Italians make good bicycles?"

"The best," I say, and he grins, and tells me *he*'s Italian, and tells me his life. They all tell me their lives, sooner or later, the lonely old men. I listen to their lives; I listen to everything very carefully. "Do you remember Bill Day?" I eventually ask them, "Guy who ran this place before me?" They do not. They try, they want to please, they are so grateful, but they do not remember him. Is that what happened to Bill Day, did he slip unremembered into the lives of these old men? I doubt it, he doesn't seem the type, but you never know. You never know, he may stop here some night, look in at the bikes in the window, come in, an old fat man, and tell me about a bike shop he had once, when he was young. Who knows?

After I close the shop, count and stash the money, set the burglar alarms, lock up, I ride one of my rental bikes home across town. If the park is still open, I ride through the park. Otherwise I circle around it to the north to reach my place on upper Broadway. I am full of fears, but I have no fear riding through the dark mugging park. Nor does street-loud Harlem frighten me. It is a beautiful place at night, broken glass and pull-tabs glittering in the softened asphalt, people gathered on stoops. The bike is not worth much, I suppose no one would kill me for it. I certainly would give it up gladly, the bike. I stop to watch a casket being carried out of a little church that is crammed between tenements. Never before have I seen a funeral at night.

My girl has moved out of our air-shafted rooming house room, and lives now with my sister on Amsterdam. I go there sometimes; she makes a late supper for me, we fight a little, I leave and ride for an hour, two hours up and down Broadway, sometimes all the way north to the river. I have a cup of coffee in the Bronx, with night owls. Often I race street kids block after block, usually beating them, for they mostly ride outlandish, long-forked imitation choppers. I am strong in my legs, though not in my arms or chest, and I am even more reckless than they, weaving around buses, running lights. I wave to them when they stop, having come to the end of their territory. I have no territory, it makes no difference where I am.

And one night, as I am about to close up, a bone-white old woman, flesh hanging like flags, comes in to sell me tickets in the Irish Sweepstakes. I buy one to get rid of her, doubting that it is legitimate. The ticket, I stare at it now, is rust-colored, with the face of a woman etched in concentric fine circles on the flimsy paper. I've never before seen a Sweeps ticket, I have no hope for this one. I stare at it now, looking for some clue.

When I have paid her for the ticket, she presses close against the counter, pressing herself towards me. She is telling me about the struggle between light and darkness. Dogs, they are on the side of darkness, devils, she says, evil. All that walk on four legs are evil, dogs are devils. And the colored, they are evil, the darkness shining in their faces. Devils everywhere, she says, beware, it is a city of danger, peril to your soul, beware.

And as I ride through dark muttering Harlem, I force myself to go very slowly, no faster than a walk, a slightly panicked walk. I search from side to side, down every street, each alley, looking for the fugitive figure of Bill Day, his shadow, watching for the night procession of mourners and the dead, darkness carrying Bill Day, his corpse, on its terrible shoulders, sweating terribly in the night.

MY WIFE HAS LEFT ME. I AM living in a little house by the river. I ride my bicycle along the river to a huge old house where a number of my friends live together. I am almost in love with one of them, a small, graceful woman with thick brown hair and gold-rimmed glasses. She and her lover have separated, he is getting ready to leave; I don't follow it all, the details of their separation. I know him only slightly.

The Cruelty of Dreams

I ride up there another day, she is there alone, doing the dishes. I touch her arm and begin to help her with the dishes. Touching her on the arm again, I ask her how things are going. It's a relief, she says, but she's lonely, has trouble sleeping. Twice I have touched her without response. I put my hand on her bare shoulder, she turns and embraces me like someone coming home. She will come and live with me in my little house by the river. She says she knew it would work out this way. I knew it too.

A few days later there is a scene of much activity in the big old house. She is moving out, moving her belongings into the little house by the river. These things, she says, carrying some boxes out of our room, do you want us to mail them to you? I'm not sure, I say, yes. These are mine? You can tell they are going to be happy together, and they treat me cordially. Where will you be going, he asks, his arm around her bare shoulders. I don't know, I say, I'll write when I get there.

They turn, return to the room where we used to live. My stuff is piled in boxes in a back hallway, hers is being loaded into a pickup truck, to be carried to his little house down the river. I lift an old-fashioned, long-handled corn popper from one of my boxes, trying to remember it. This is mine?

Welfare Island

IT WAS THE LAST WEEK BEFORE I left New York, and her, to begin graduate school in the Midwest. It was the end of everything. It was after the end, in fact, but still close enough to be our period punctuation. We were nice to each other all that week, because it was over and we were still there, walking through it.

I had quit my summer job, and she had never shown up for hers very regularly anyway. She was often sick, and the downtown department store where she worked didn't seem to mind. And so we were spending the day wandering around the city as we had not done all summer. We lived on the west side, near Columbia, and were now walking in the glamorous east. We had lunch at a fancy bar and grill, ignoring for once the cost of what we ate and drank, a little surprised at how easy it was. When she had visited the ladies' room (she was always looking for a ladies' room those days) we wandered toward the river.

We stood on a concrete platform, traffic moving underneath us, and looked out at Welfare Island (since renamed "Roosevelt"). We had never been there. Because I love islands I said we should cross over and look around. There was a new fountain somewhere on Welfare Island, I had read, and I wanted to see it.

We were near the Queensboro Bridge, which, crossing from Manhattan, drops a great leg onto the thin strip of river-shaped land before passing on to Queens. Yet we had to walk a long way back before we came to where the bridge approach begins. We crossed warily the two lanes of westward traffic; a guard-rail; two lanes of traffic moving east. Even after living in the city for months, she was the worst person in traffic I've ever known. You had to half-drag her across, for she would just freeze. We made it and started up the long incline on the narrow metal footpath. Before we were above the river itself we were alarmingly far from the ground. We paused to look down at a brick smokestack that towered up to us, and beyond us, from some tiny sheds and warehouses.

The smotheringly massive tower seemed to move against the moving water. To shake myself from the sight I grabbed her and staggered back to the railing that separated us from the oblivious rush of cars. "It's falling!" I screamed, feeling better as I felt her shudder against me. Even after the first startle, I was scaring her. It was so easy, I couldn't help it sometimes. Holding her in a close, cold, dramatic clutch I narrated a swaying, grinding prelude and the great, groaning crash of those unthinkable millions of bricks, crushing build ings and buses for blocks, falling on the town like a fire-hardened tornado. "If it had only fallen into the river," I sadly reflected, staring down into the gaping, smoking black pit, orange fires licking up, astonished at the sudden light. "So many lives would have been spared," I said, "and so much less mess to clean up." She nodded vaguely, staring at nothing. Already the brief feeling of power was fading. "But look!" I cheered, pointing up the river, "the excursion boat was spared!" We watched a Circle Line boat churn peacefully south, ignorant of the disaster it had so narrowly escaped.

"Come on," I said, drawing her up the bridge once more, "I can't look at it anymore." She laughed then. She didn't always. But we were alone, of course; no one was there to complicate the game. We were invisible to the cars that rushed across the bridge, somewhat below our walk. Reality was in control.

When the arc of the bridge reached its apex we looked down dizzily at the island. Rusty, treacherous-looking stairs like an old fire escape led down to the building squatting under the central piers. We zigzagged down, once having to use a ladder between landings, three-fourths of the height of the bridge before finding ourselves in an echoing, gloomy building, empty, unaccountable, crusted everywhere with layers and layers of institutional paint. We stood in an empty hallway, lost, until an old man's voice called to us from the dark, "Going down." There was no other direction. We found the elevator shaft from which he had called out, got in, and rode down in silence with the short, shriveled man. Surely we were not supposed to be there, I whispered, and any questions about where we were would give us away. The old man hardly looked at us as we stepped out and walked toward the light. "I think we're trespassing," I said. "We could get into some real trouble." She was trying to ignore me. "I'm serious," I said. "Do you have a record?"

"Don't," she said, so low I scarcely heard. "Don't, please."

We walked out of the musty building, past dripping, crusted pipes and a rust-stained porcelain drinking fountain, out into the girdered shadow of the bridge. We were on the west side of the island, facing Manhattan. A long asphalt walk ran along the water's edge southward, cracked by broad-bladed grasses. Along this promenade, bench after bench faced the city, silent with separation, across the iron railing. The sides of the benches were eroded pebbly concrete; the backs and seats were gray, splintering boards, only half there. "Like us," I said.

I thought the fountain was at the south end of the island. We walked along before the benches, looking across the choppy water. Behind us, massive brick buildings towered menacingly, blank-eyed, roofs grown a deep arsenic green, heavily chimneyed, elaborately gabled. The lower doors and windows were sealed with galvanized steel. We walked around these haunted, deeply disturbed buildings and saw that they were posted with "condemned" notices. "Condemned," I said. "They're out-and-out damned."

"You're so clever," she said.

We found an overgrown grove of cedars with barely visible stone paths wandering in and out. We found rusty gangs of tractor-drawn mowers, and a wrecked fleet of wheelchairs, rusting, the rubber of their tires crumbling. I found one wheelchair all of wood, in good shape still, and this I pulled out of the thistles and sunflowers onto the sunny walkway by the water. I did not tell her what I was thinking. I did not say what I thought about her and this ruined refuge from a world visible but grown silent across the water. I did the only thing I could. I sat down in the wheelchair and became hunched over, chilled, trembling, coughing weakly, waiting for nurse her to push me.

She went along with it, surprisingly, and then was taking her turn as the invalid when I spotted another Circle Line tour steaming past, some of its passengers watching us. I waved cheerfully and told her in a loud, encouraging voice, "There, Dear, be brave! Wave to the nice people on the nice boat! Someday perhaps you will be able to take a nice boat ride too!" She didn't laugh this time. She stood up abruptly, jolting the old chair, and walked away without speaking. "Praise the Lord!" I shouted to the passengers of the Circle Line tour, "Praise the Lord! The doctors said she would never walk again! Praise the Lord!" A few uncertain cheers and thin clapping came across the water.

The boat drew away finally. I sent the wheelchair spinning into a tangle of lilacs, caught up, and walked beside her. "Nice recovery, kid," I said finally.

She turned to me. "Can't we just walk, for once? Can't we just be together, see the same things, and leave it at that?" For a while we just walked. "What is this place?" she asked. "What was it?"

"Hospital, I think. TB sanitarium. Blood spots on my pillow."

"Not a mental hospital?" she asked. "I think I saw bars on some of the windows."

"No, Baby," I said, putting my arm around her shoulders. "It's just a TB hospital, a dead one, coughed up its last lung years ago." I led her away from the monstrous dark buildings and tangled paths, down from the end of the promenade onto the actual river bank. Soon the buildings were hidden by the trees.

The shore turned in at the tip of the narrow island. There was an area of barren sand and rocks, and from beside a little gray structure a narrow tower of water, a hundred and fifty, two hundred feet tall, stood over us, its top breaking into clouds, the spray pounding down upon the graveled beach. A wind carried the mist outward toward the river, and we approached as close as we dared. The power and continuous violence of the eruption was shocking, exhilarating.

She was tired from all the walking we had done and after a minute she moved off and sat down on the stones at the water's edge. She already wanted to go back, but she wouldn't say so. I climbed around a little, throwing rocks at the steel-hard spout of water. Finally I sat down beside her, breathing hard.

"I wish I had known you when you were a little boy," she said. She was always saying things like that, hopeless things.

"I haven't changed so much," I said. "I thought that was one of your big gripes, that I've never grown up." I had not meant to speak to her that way, but she was always saying hopeless things.

She didn't seem to mind. "It must have been different, though," she said. "You do crazy things now, and there's a kind of desperation behind it. It must have been innocent, once." That was another thing she did — turn her analysis against me.

"It was always like it is now," I said. The fountain had dropped for some reason, so I went over to see where it came from, exactly, and had to run like hell to get away when it suddenly erupted again. I didn't want to sit down wet, and it was starting to get late. Since we had so far explored only a part of the island I gave her my hand and drew her up. She was still tired, but I wanted to see the whole island.

We walked north again, this time along the Queens side, and looked again at the great condemned buildings. They were the same horror from every angle. I would not have gone inside them for anything. "Let's go inside one of those,"

I suggested, watching her covertly. She shuddered, a real shudder such as you seldom see. I had to laugh. I would not have gone inside for fame or fortune, but I acted disappointed at her unwillingness to explore the horrible ruins.

When we were almost past, she asked in a strange, distant voice, "Why are there bars, then?"

"What?"

"Why are there bars on the windows, if this wasn't a mental hospital?"

"I don't know," I answered, annoyed. "Maybe to protect the consumptive little girls from rapists coming over from Manhattan when nothing's doing in Central Park." She drew away. "Hell," I said, "I don't know. I didn't see any bars."

"I saw them," she said. She was always seeing hopeless things, and that used to really depress me.

"I wonder why there's no one around," I said. "If I were a kid living in the city, I'd come here all the time." The thought made me feel fine. "I'd carry a sword and drop on the rapists like a plague and be a hero to the little bird-throated coughing girls." I poked her on the arm, and she sighed. I had to laugh.

We passed under the bridge again. I looked up at the distant web of welded steel, trying to imagine ourselves creeping like flies along the nearly invisible walkway. It made me dizzy. I dropped down flat on my back, my arms spread wide, to get the full effect. She strode on, ignoring me, ignoring the bridge that filled the entire sky. I forgot her for a moment, then, while tiny cars drifted across my face.

I had to get up, finally, and ran to catch up with her. She ignored me, ignored the newer buildings, apparently still in use — low brick buildings with a few cars parked outside them, and loading docks in back — ignored everything until we entered another wild stretch and came upon a little chapel, almost lost in the close-growing silver maples and ropes of morning glories. She took my arm, obviously enchanted, and we approached the little brick building feeling like children in a fairy tale.

"It's like something in a book," she whispered. Most of its windows were gone. We circled about to the front and climbed up to the open door to look inside. It was disappointing after the picturesque, viny exterior. There were no pews, the floor was littered with plaster and other trash, and a piano lay on its side, smashed open.

"I have to go to the bathroom," she whispered, disengaging herself from my arm. "There's some sort of basement," I said. "Do you want me to go with you?"

"No," she answered, embarrassed, "stay here. I'll be back in a moment." I listened to her hesitant steps, waiting for a muffled scream. Nothing. I walked around the piano. "Lori + Max — 69ers" I read from the spray-painted wall. The strings of the piano, rusted against the gold sounding-board, caught my eye. I ran my fingers across them, and the desolated chapel echoed with the music of horror movies. I picked up a crooked, dismembered key, its ivory still adhering, and ran it lightly, then hard, across the wires. The weird sound filled the room, haunting it suddenly. I did it again and again, thinking how spooky it must sound to her, abstractedly squatting somewhere in the dark below, when she came up suddenly behind me, scaring me a little. I raked the key across the strings once more, then tossed it away. "Let's get out of here," I said, enchantment gone.

"You know," I said as we walked away, "that was pretty bad, desecrating a church like that, pissing in it."

"Don't," she said. "Don't, don't."

"I mean it," I said, "that's worse than blasphemy, isn't it?"

"Don't," she said, "please please don't." The walk we were following no longer hugged the river's edge, but wandered somewhat inland. I wasn't sure how far we were from the north end. It was getting dark and even I was getting pretty tired, though I would have loved to have circled the entire island. When we came upon a road that crossed the island and seemed to turn south again, we took it, trudging along, mostly in silence.

"I would like to live here," she said after a while, "in a little vine-covered cottage, half-hidden in the side of a small hill, with no one to bother me. No one. I'd come and go as I pleased."

Somehow this was aimed at me. "You'd go screaming crazy here after one night," I said. "It's getting dark now; how do you like it? Do you want me to leave you here?"

She lifted her chin. "Is that what you think?" she asked.

"What?"

"That I'm going to go crazy. I think that's pretty ironic, coming from you."

"Cut it out," I told her. "You're not going to go crazy. Let's just get out of here." We walked faster; she was always lagging behind me by a few steps. We were a longer ways past the bridge than I had thought. We saw no one, and the parked cars we had seen earlier were gone. It was almost dark by the time we reached the enigmatic building that was our gateway to the bridge. It was dark. We tried the door. It was locked. A little beyond, invisible, were the great ruined buildings. I could not stand to think about them, the little black rooms with rat-gnawed mattresses, the corridors, the missing stairways, the locked and the unlocked doors.

"Now we're in for it, Baby," I said. "We're going to have to swim for it before the spooks come out." I started taking off my shoes. She suddenly sat down at the side of the road and started to cry. I had almost never seen her cry, and it was upsetting. She always remained tightly dry-eyed, no matter how bad it was. I uncomfortably put my arm around her. "Baby," I pleaded, "Baby, please."

"I have to get out of here," she moaned. "I can't stand it here. I have to get out of here." I tried to smother her cries in my arms, but didn't know what to do. There had to be another way off the island. We had seen cars. But I could see there was no bridge on the Manhattan side except the now-inaccessible monster soaring over us, and we had noticed nothing on the Queens side. I crouched beside her, rocking her in my arms, trying to get some warmth from her. My stomach crawled every time I thought about those dead dark rooms, those rotten mattresses.

And then two teen-age boys rode by on bicycles out of the gloom as if it were part of the natural world. They told us that within a half hour a bus would come by which could take us into Queens. After they left she sat beside me, grown still and passive. In a short time the bus came, an old yellow school bus that serviced whatever part of the institution still functioned. It circled the island in the darkness and left by a low bridge we had somehow overlooked, having perhaps turned inland before coming to it.

We had to pay nothing to get off Welfare Island. "This is too easy," I said. "We should of swum." The driver dropped us off somewhere in Queens, telling us what bus would get us back to Manhattan. I bought Italian ices from a street vendor while we waited. The bus came and we headed back. We sat beside each other silently, the paper cones sticky in our hands. I leaned over her and looked down as the bus rattled effortlessly across the towering, impassive bridge. I could see nothing of the island and sat back again.

"They are going to tear all that down in a few years," I said. "They will change the name of the island from Welfare to Roosevelt." She was staring out the window. "They are going to build a self-contained, luxury high-rise community there," I told her, "and connect it to Manhattan with a tram line."

I looked at her. She had not heard. I had not spoken. I knew none of that, then, and did not know where she would go and where and when we would meet again, three times after that summer, and how hopeless and helpless we both had been from before the beginning of whatever had begun and ended.

"You are going to be unhappy for years," I did not tell her. "I am going to fail again and again to understand."

SHE HAS HAD A SHORT STORY published in *Harpers*. They are paying her a great deal of money for it, who has never been paid more than fifteen dollars for anything she has written. Usually she has been paid in copies. They have some friends over to celebrate. He is very hearty, and drinks most of the good scotch it was his idea to serve.

A short time later she is appointed director of the state Poets in the Schools program, a well-paying job. They will now be able to move out of her parents' home and rent a small place of their own. He suggests they celebrate alone this time, but they can hardly avoid a housewarming for their literary friends, especially the Poets in the Schools. He starts to spend a lot of time with some people he knew from graduate school.

And then he gets a state arts grant to finish a prose poem on the Sioux uprising, a poem on which he has not worked for several years. He says he wants to play it down, but she insists on a real bash in his honor. At the party she is radiant and tells everyone how relieved she is that finally he has gotten the break he deserves. It was getting a little awkward, she laughs. His friends from graduate school surround him all evening, drinking heavily.

And then she wins the Yale Younger Poets Award. And then Viking Press accepts her book of translations of Southwest Indian myths. It is nominated for a National Book Award, and their friends say, it has been a good year for them.

The Siege

WITH A CRY OF PAIN ALLEN jerked his hand back from the blazing chrome of his car, baking at the curb beside a broad, low-cut stump that had been stripped of bark to the soil. After wrapping the handle with the tail of his shirt he managed to get the door open, then slid into the stale blast of heat and started the old Volvo, being careful to touch as little metal as possible. He drove fifty feet forward and parked again, just ahead of the shade cast by the massive oak that sheltered his front lawn. By the time the shadow moved past the car again, the sun would have lost some of its fury. He burned himself again as he got out and cursed softly to himself.

As he turned toward his house a voice called to him from one of the many gable windows in the high-pitched slate roof. Then a second voice screamed, "We're up here, Al," and two small boys, about four- and six-years-old, stuck their heads out the gable window. A window in another angle of the roof quivered in the sun, slammed up suddenly and on the rebound smashed down again, breaking one of the small panes. The window rose again, this time more slowly, grasped by small hands. A girl a few years older than the older boy appeared in the window, jammed a board in as a prop, then looked down at Allen apologetically. "Sorry about the window, Allen. It wasn't really my fault." "What's going on?" he asked, shading his eyes. "How did you guys get up there?" "We're getting some junk for a fort," the girl said, and the older boy, Rick, appeared beside her. "Annie found a trapdoor in the back. We borrowed your ladder and got it open. The stuff up here is perfect for our fort." "I'll bet," Allen muttered, his eyes watering from looking into the sun. "Why do you need a fort, anyway? Are we under attack?" The girl gave a weary toss of her head and disappeared back into the attic. The smaller boy, Lewis, crowed from the first window again, "We're up here, Al!" "Yeah," Allen said, rubbing the tears out of his eyes, "you sure are."

These were Gail's kids, running wild in his huge, mostly unrestored house. It was an asymmetrical building of dusty, red-orange brick and orange stone, with pillars supporting the roof of a portico that half-surrounded the building. Elaborately pierced stone arches leaped from pillar to pillar, and two stories of tall windows and a three-quarter-round tower rose over the broad porch to a tangle of steeply pitched dormers, gables, cones, and turrets, all sharing an appalling weight of pink and gray slate shingles.

Allen rejoined Gail in the kitchen, behind the great round living and dining room which formed the first level of the restored tower. She was sitting at the enameled table, reading, drinking iced tea. "Are they killing themselves?" she asked as he got a beer from the refrigerator. "It sounded like they broke something." "They're getting stuff for a fort," he said. Looking out the back window he could see where they had already accumulated a pile of old drop cloths in the weed-grown vacant lot beside the house. "Tell me," he said, "why is it that everything they build is a fort?"

Sometimes he thought of her children as creatures from another planet, which seemed ironic to Gail, who saw so much of the child in him. When he thought of being a father to them, the strangeness literally shook him. "They already have a father," Gail had snapped at him once when he was worrying over the prospect. "Which makes it that much worse," he had groaned, watching her lips grow white with impatience. He had no children of his own, had practiced contraception until he was an expert, until his lovemaking was a masterpiece of contraception. Gail had been pleased by his concern when they first became lovers, though it struck her now as being a little extreme.

"Why don't they call them shacks or something?" "What did you call them when you were a kid?" she asked, keeping her place in the book. She pushed her glasses up on her nose and looked at him with a little smile. He thought about it for a few moments and then answered, "We called them forts."

Something crashed high above them, and a shrill, rhythmic

wail started up. "Oh my god," Gail said. "They've brought the roof down on Lewis. How do you get up there, Allen?" He shrugged, "I don't really know." They went out to the front hallway, found a door open to one of several staircases leading up to the various levels of the monstrous house. Following the rise and fall of Lewis's cries they climbed two flights of dark, littered stairs, saw light at the end of a high-ceilinged hallway, and found the collapsed stepladder and a pile of debris on the floor. Annie, Rick, and Lewis leaned over the edge of the trapdoor. Lewis stopped crying as soon as he saw them, for he was not hurt. He had simply thought that he was trapped forever in the dark attic. The smell of musty trapped heat filtered down with clouds of dust from the trapdoor as Allen and Gail steadied the ladder and helped the children down. Rick first handed down an old wicker baby buggy and Annie was awkward with an armload of big books, all of which turned out to be in German.

As the children began dragging off their plunder, Allen climbed up to replace the trapdoor. From his perch on top of the ladder he looked around, then pulled himself the rest of the way into the attic. Gail objected, but then followed him. The attic held what all attics hold, though it held more than usual, covered with an unusually thick layer of very fine, black powder. As if in a daze Allen and Gail began going through the old clothes and shoes and boxes of books and mysterious partial machinery and broken sports equipment and bundles of indecipherable brittle letters. They went through them the way all adults do — that is, like children, though children usually work through an attic with a greater sense of purpose.

In a few minutes they were filthy, but it didn't matter since they were wearing work clothes anyway. Gail looked up from a yellowed photo album and sighed. "We're supposed to be painting, Allen." When they finished fixing up the three rooms in the east wing of the house there would be room for the five of them to live together. And when their respective divorces were accomplished she would sell the little tract house that neither she nor her husband wanted, and she and Allen would or would not get married, and they would live together in the big house, still half a ruin, and room by room they would return it to something like its former glory. They weren't progressing very rapidly, Gail thought from time to time. Sometimes when she watched him fool around it seemed as if they might as well be making plans for living in a tree house.

Ignoring her suggestion that they get back to work, Allen went to the window in the front of the attic which Annie had propped open. Leaning out he could see the three children making another trip between the porch and their fort beside the house. He called to them, "We're up here, Lewis!" The little boy looked up and clapped with delight. Awkwardly Allen thrust one leg and half his upper body out the narrow window. In a high falsetto he screamed, "My baby's in that buggy! I'm going to jump!" Lewis laughed till he could hardly stand, but Annie and Rick looked at each other and shrugged. "I mean it!" Allen shouted, feeling for the steeply slanted roof with his foot. "Cut it out, Al," Rick called up to him. "Everybody is going to think you're crazy." There was a pause when everything hung in a balance. "O.K.," Allen said at last and pulled himself back into the attic. He went over and sat on a carton beside Gail. "That Lewis is a good kid." Gail laughed, put her arm around his shoulders. "He'll be older than you too in a couple of years." Allen brushed dirt from the wooden rim of a bicycle wheel he had found by the window and tried to turn the axle. It moved stiffly in the ancient, congealed grease. When he looked around for the rest of the bicycle he found only a pile of cracked, narrow tires.

"Let's go downstairs," he suggested, "while the kids are busy outside." "All right." Then, "Oh. Allen, I feel funny about it, with the kids around." He thrust his chin out stubbornly. "We'll make a fort. The circular stairs can be de-

fended." "No, Sweetheart," she said. "They'd lay a terrible
siege if they thought any funny business was going on."
"Well," he said. "Well well." She rose, went over to him,
took the wheel and laid it aside. "I'm a mess," she said after a
minute. "Can you taste the dust?" "Ashes to ashes," he said.
"Dust to dust." Gently she disengaged herself from him and
held him at arms' length. "Allen, next weekend Steve gets the
kids. We can be alone all weekend." "You're not working
next Saturday?" "We'll have all Saturday evening and all
Sunday." "I have to play for early mass," he said. "We'll have
all Saturday night, then. Oh come on, this won't last forever.
We have to be patient or we'll ruin it." "That's easy for you to
say," Allen muttered. She clapped her hands in his face.
"Come on, sublimate. If we get some work done we'll finally
have someplace to stash the little beggars. You want that,
don't you?" "Sure I do," he said, flushing a deep sudden red
that made Gail look at him sharply before turning toward the
door.

Allen helped her as she crawled out the trapdoor and down
the stepladder. Before climbing down himself he went back
and closed the window with the broken pane, then closed the
other window and looked for something to plug the hole. He
took one of the long dresses that were packed into a steamer
trunk and stuffed as much of it as he could through the opening. Looking one last time through the dusty window he saw
the cathedral looming grayly at the edge of the bluff, vaguely
distorted by the rippled glass and seeming gauzy and insub-
stantial through the film of dust. Something from a neutral-
tinted dream.

Gail and Allen worked the rest of the afternoon steaming
and scraping old wallpaper from the largest of the three
rooms in the east wing. They worked steadily at the tedious
job until it was supper time. When they had started supper,
Allen went out to get the children. He paused for a moment
beside the oak on his front lawn, the only tree left on the
block. There was a spot at the base of the tree where Allen

often sat, comfortable in a basin formed by a great looping root that had been worn smooth by his seat. There was a sense of permanence in the shadow of the oak that was lacking in the house, as solid and massive as it was. Sometimes he fell asleep there, sitting with his back against the rough bark. Once, having gone out to wait for stars, he woke in the early morning and found himself there, his face cold with dew. His legs, paralyzed with sleep, gave way when he tried to stand, causing him to fall back against the trunk. He was clutching the tree for support when the paperboy coasted by. "Rough night?" the boy had asked him, and he had not been able to think of an answer.

Now as he crossed the lawn to the tree the grass under his feet crackled. Though it was only the middle of June, the grass was parched yellow in the third summer of drought. Only in the shade of the oak was the grass green and soft, for Allen watered the tree furtively at night, violating the city's ban. For a moment now he sank down near the buttressed trunk, lay on his back, and stared up through the crooked limbs and dark glossy foliage. He could hear the kids talking from time to time as their voices rose shrilly over the drone of cicadas. "You *can't* be king, Annie," Rick kept insisting. "You can't be."

Allen rose and found the girl and the two boys in a field filled with half-buried brick walls and lines of stone and disintegrating concrete. Annie stuck her head out of the structure they had assembled from the old baby buggy, some boxes, a patched tarpaulin, and cement-crusted lumber. "Check out our fort, Allen," she invited. He squatted down and looked in; Lewis was eating graham crackers, and Rick was digging with a knife beneath the buggy. A pleasant light pierced the gloom of the crazy structure. Allen tried to crawl in, but there was not enough room for him even when Annie crawled out to make way for him. When his back dragged against the board supporting the tarp Lewis shrieked with surprise and alarm. Rick ordered Allen out. "You're busting our fort, Al!" he complained. "O.K.," Allen said, "O.K.," and backed out carefully.

"Why do you call it a fort?" he asked Annie as she adjusted the paint-stiff tarp on the balanced framework. She looked at him curiously, and then said, "Because it is one. A fort is what it is." "It's sort of a little house, isn't it?" he suggested. "Sort of a tent?" "It's a fort," she said and ducked through the canvas door. Allen stood there, looking down at the fort, and then said through the baby buggy wall that they should come in for supper. When there was no response he walked back toward the house.

2

"Goat hair," she said. His hand drew back involuntarily from the saddle-shaped bundle of coarse yarn suspended from the ceiling of the shop. He had not heard her approach, for a radio somewhere in the building was playing a loud revival hymn, blasting it out. "Funny stuff, isn't it," she observed, giving the object a little poke with her fingers to set it swinging. "Smells awful when it's humid." "It's bad enough now." It made his skin crawl. "I sort of like it," she said. "It's Turkish, we just got it in."

He walked beside her through the narrow aisles, past tall wooden shelves stuffed snug with skeins of yarn and tubes wound with lovely cotton and linen thread and barrels of unspun cotton and wool and loops of mysterious bark-like fiber. She leaned against the big loom that stood beside the counter. It was the first thing one noticed on entering the shop; Allen found it strangely compelling.

"You're early," she said. "Well, I was in the neighborhood.

I played for a wedding this afternoon." Which explained his
dark suit. He reached into the frame of the loom and drew his
fingers across the harp of the prepared warp. It was disap-
pointingly soft, slack, noiseless as an owl's wing. He drew his
palm across the threads and felt a pleasant tickling of the
cotton. "Can you work this thing?" he asked. She slid herself
onto the bench before the partly rolled cloth that curved up
over a bar at her breast and then became mere warp as it
flowed into the confusion of suspended, eyeletted wires. She
cranked the warp tight, clicking a ratchet, as her feet found the
pedals. She picked up the wooden shuttle with its slim reel of
weft and sailed it across the level plain of warp, a shed of
alternating threads sloping above it.

The position was familiar to Allen, though he did not know
the names of either the parts or the processes involved. With a
kind of harmony that was all too rare between them he could
feel her hands and feet, their attention, as his own. The
rhythm was hypnotic: swish, thump, clack following themselves steadily. He watched the pale gold cloth, a yard wide,
grow away from her against the steady beating back of the
heavy-framed metal reed, the shuttle floating from hand to
hand. When she stopped suddenly, he followed the movement
for another beat, then straightened. "What are you making?"
"Nothing," she said. "We just have this warped up so people
can try it out."

He began examining the maple machinery of the levers and
pedals that lowered and lifted the four harnesses with such
primitive elegance. He tried to imagine threading the hundreds of warp threads into their proper heddle and reed open-
ings, but the prospect alarmed him so, he tried not to think
about it. Gail leaned back from the breast beam and ran her
fingers idly across the new cloth, pale gold and dark brown,
that was not going to be anything. Allen was aware of her at
that moment with an almost painful intensity, felt her eyes
smiling from behind the big glasses, her pale skin, her heavy
black hair, her large features. She often watched him that way,

but for him the experience was very rare, and not entirely pleasant.

Gail seemed only half aware of Allen watching her among the massy cones of thread, the polished wood warping boards and Danish looms, the shuttles and the spinning wheels. Then a young man with hair like an angry red cloud came into the shop, and Gail went to wait on him. It took them a long time to get straight what he wanted. The skeins of goat-hair yarn hung oppressively above Allen's head and he kept ducking, needlessly, under the supplies suspended from the ceiling as he moved away. When Gail finally came back, Allen said, "Let's go." She put away some leftover thread, half-listening to the cracking, resonant voice of the radio preacher invoking the end of the world in a purge of Pentecostal fires. As the preacher gave an address for contributions and a free pamphlet explaining the sign of the coming of Christ, Allen said, "Well?"

"I don't usually close for another hour, Allen. Do you mind waiting that long?" He shrugged his shoulders, disappointed, but then sat down at the loom and had her show him what to do. Although he left a wretched, ragged selvedge and forgot the order of what he was doing and repeatedly undid what he had just done, when she came and told him that she was about to close up he was almost reluctant to leave. He walked down the block to pick up a bottle of wine. When he returned she was sitting in the window well of the darkened shop, writing in a notebook.

As they drove along Summit Avenue the thick-boled lilacs that had once bloomed gloriously on the median strip appeared drought-shriveled, and the ghost of the lost arch of elms cast a deep, forgotten shadow over the hot street. The houses were big, solid houses of the 1890s, houses of the wealthy, but set close to one another, huddled as close together as decorum allowed. Allen compared them idly with his own isolated house. Only here and there was there space sufficient for a new home to spring up between two dark old mansions.

As the avenue approached the downtown area the houses took on the proportions of small, thick castles drooping ponderously over the round lip of bluff that dropped breakneck to the ancient flood bed of the Mississippi. In a loop of the river lay the banks, insurance companies, and abandoned stores of the City of St. Paul, hungover with the dust pall of construction. A new freeway was cutting the city apart once more, there were huge holes and flat wastes where a "city center" was to be built, and the canyon of a future underground mall gaped wide. Thin sweet smoke rose from a steam-generating incinerator across the river, burning the last of the city's elms. The avenue followed the bluff as it curved north to the bulky gray cathedral. The cathedral sat at the very lip of the steeply rounded bluff, the green copper dome brooding down upon the state capitol complex and its dome of white and gold.

Allen turned off just before reaching the cathedral, drove along a side street for two blocks, and parked across the street from his house. When they got out there was a hum in the air. The light was the heartbreaking, beautiful light that hangs about old demolished buildings and vacant lots. Allen took Gail's arm, holding her close to him as they started across the street. She stopped and drew him back to the curb as an old man on a bicycle rode past. The old man, about seventy, portly, bald, with a gray goatee, pedalled past on an ancient balloon-tired lady's bicycle. He steered with one hand while the other supported a four-foot length of air duct that lay across the big wire basket. He seemed not to notice them, though Gail smiled and waved, but rode by at a stately, even pace, heading toward the cathedral down the brick-paved, crooked alley — Maiden Lane. "He's a scavenger," Allen said, "I see him hauling all sorts of junk."

Gail gazed after the old man as they crossed the street, and laughed, "It's some neighborhood." It was. The neighborhood was marked by the sunny openness that surrounds abandoned brick warehouses and factories at the edges of dying towns, airy webs of broken windows in broad skylights, grass cracking concrete, foundations and fields making peace.

But this, of course, was the heart of the city, a small soft hollow among mansions of the twenties and teens and turn of the century, an island of openness isolated from the gathering ghetto by the drop of bluffs on one side, impregnable freeways on two others, with the cathedral and its outbuildings and parking lots arrayed on top of the bluff. Something had driven the wealthy families from the block, leaving it hollow and secure.

The cathedral stood at the opposite end of Maiden Lane from Allen's place, across a parking lot from the end of the broad, brief alley cut on the bias past the junky back yard of an old house with children, a little white house and garage with an old man sweeping up, and an inexplicable warehouse or factory of yellow brick, its boarded-up or barred windows too high off the ground for anyone to look in.

Allen's father-in-law, a city politician and real estate developer, had given the half-ruined mansion to Elizabeth and him as a wedding present. The old man had owned the property at the end of Maiden Lane for years without giving it a thought, until the rough joke of it occurred to him when his only daughter, whom he scarcely knew, was about to be married. "He sent in a renovation crew a few weeks before the wedding," Allen told Gail as they stood on the porch, both reluctant to leave the glowing early evening and the cool of the oak's shade. "They got the first two levels of the tower and the kitchen into livable shape, then left it. He didn't want to spoil our fun in restoring the place. Elizabeth never forgave him. That was five years ago."

Except for the broad tower that swelled out toward Maiden Lane and the cathedral, and a portion of the house around the back, all the lower windows and many above were sealed with plywood. The mortar about the base of the red stone pillars was crumbling alarmingly, and the portico was littered with empty and full sacks of cement, tarpaulins, and crusted lumber. "I've become addicted to the old monster," Allen said. He picked up a curved pointing tool and scraped at the loose mortar between two stones.

"Listen, I'm starting to get hungry," Gail said, and they went in. "I'll cook," Allen announced, disappearing through the swinging doors of the compact, odd-angled kitchen which extended back from the tower into the bulk of the house. Gail stood for a moment in the middle of the almost round room. There was an old couch, a wooden swivel chair with the varnish rubbed from its arms, back, and seat, and a long wooden chest, about the size of a coffin. A battered baby grand piano spread itself sturdily into the arc of windows.

It was not her house — the thought struck her without warning, though she had been there many times before and had always felt comfortable enough. I should feel by now that I belong, she thought, but there was something inescapably removed about it. It belongs to Allen, she thought, for he loves it, and he loves me. He loves me and he loves the kids and we will belong here and it will be our house. She liked the house, had worked on it gladly. It's not mine, she thought again. It's not Elizabeth's, but it's not mine. It's not mine. She felt herself trapped inside the words, fastened to them, which could at any moment change to something worse. She shook herself involuntarily, then, like a wet dog, physically shaking off the words. And then she felt better, though still uneasy.

"Allen," she called, "do you need any help?" She stood at the base of the carved, darkly polished oak staircase that circled up through an octagonal, wood-framed opening in the ceiling. The oiled wood of the bannister seemed almost alive under her hand. "Allen?" She heard opening and slamming drawers and a rummaging of silverware and small kitchen utensils as Allen searched impatiently for the one corkscrew that really worked, the one he could never find. He had gone through all likely drawers and was beginning a second round. He found the one that tore up corks, rusting in the draining rack, and kept looking. The good corkscrew was in the glove compartment of his car; he was about to remember it.

Gail climbed the winding staircase through the heavy wooden frame into the second story of the tower. The bannister coiled into a protective railing around the opening in the floor of the crowded room, smaller than the one below by the depth of a semicircle of closets. A bathroom door stood open at the far end of the room, which was where she was headed. To the right of the bathroom door, against the one flat wall of the room, stood another piano, an upright. A tall brass bed stood directly above the baby grand a floor below, and in the middle of the room, like an island, there was an enormous black desk, dangerously connected with the wall by the extension cord from an elaborate draughtsman's lamp.

Gail circled down the stairs again, sliding outward against the bannister. Allen had to dodge back out of the way as she flew off the last step. He nearly dropped one of the glasses, and a few drops of the pale wine slopped onto the floor. "Where were you?" he asked. "Allen, why do you have two pianos?" she asked, taking one of the glasses. "This one was Elizabeth's, the one upstairs is mine, I guess. It was up there when we moved in. I don't know how they got it up there." He gestured toward the winding staircase. He sat on the piano bench, she in the swivel chair, which creaked like a wooden ship under sail.

There was an antique walnut table drawn compactly into itself standing behind the staircase. When he had finished his glass of wine, Allen pulled the table into the open and spread its leaves, pleased as always by the elegance of its sliding and hinged expansion. They each carried out a chair from the kitchen; Gail set the table while Allen drew things from oven and stove top.

They ate the broiled trout and asparagus and buttered noodles and talked about the house, then about her children. "Do they mind me?" Allen asked. "You know they love you, Allen, what a question." "I mean," he said, "do they think I've come between you and Steve?" She smiled. "In a way you have, you know. I probably wouldn't have kicked him out if I hadn't fallen in love with you." "I wish you wouldn't talk like that," he complained, clicking his fork sharply against a plate. "It's the truth," she said. "It's not your fault, there's no fault involved. The kids are fair. They know what it was like between Steve and me toward the end, they were there." "I feel like a cad, sometimes," he said. "Sometimes you are a cad," she said, unsure why she was pushing at him this way. But when he drew back into himself she reached for his hand and held it. "We're doing the right thing, Allen. But we have to keep our eyes open, we mustn't pretend." "That's easy for you to say," he replied. She took her hand away and laid it quietly on her lap. "It's not so easy," she said.

There was still some daylight, but since the room faced east it was already pretty dark. Allen didn't seem to notice, and began talking about his plans for restoring the brickwork. Gail rose and switched on a floor lamp as he talked. When they finally carried their dishes into the kitchen, his plate was still half full. Gail had finished.

After setting the coffee pot on the stove they took what was left of their wine into the living room and sat down together on the nappy brown couch. She kissed him lightly, but did not put down her glass. "It was a lovely meal," she told him. He nodded vaguely and put his arms around her. She sat quietly. "Well," he said, drawing back a little when she did not respond, "shall we compare divorces? How is your divorce these days?" Gail stood up and walked to the windows that curved out around the piano. "Why don't you play something for me," she said. She leaned back and through her raised glass looked at the scrubby lawn, now almost dark. He's so terribly young, she thought. It was not always appealing.

Allen went to the piano and sat down. "Are you putting me

off, by any chance? We should get to know each other again,
you know." "Right," she said. "Now come on, play something." He began to fool around, stringing together sharp,
comical little phrases. There was an edginess in his playing,
but that was something that was always there, a matter of
rhythm more than key. The piano was slightly out of tune —
just the right amount, he thought, relaxing a little.

Gail lounged back against the piano and from time to time
rested a sandaled foot on the low ledge of the window bay.
She wondered if her kids were outside still, and recalled with a
strange smile that tomorrow was Father's Day. She usually
liked Allen's playing, though she knew nothing about music.
She watched the bit of gray cathedral visible down Maiden
Lane disappear and saw, under the great oak before the house,
a squirrel that was working late. When the light was nearly
gone she fished a spiral notepad and a pencil out of the bag she
had left on the piano and wrote something. Returning pencil
and pad to her bag, she turned to him.

"It's getting dark," she said. "Would you like some more
light? I can move the lamp." He shook his head almost invisibly. "What did you write just now?" he asked. "Nothing. A
few words." "You wrote me a poem once," he recalled. "I
didn't understand it." He kept playing, softly, as she sat down
beside him on the piano bench, her arm resting lightly on his
shoulder. "What did you write?" he asked again. "It's just one
line: 'He makes his scalloped way across the lawn.' That's
all." "Who he?" "Squirrel," she laughed. "Think of the corny
rhymes for 'lawn.'" "There's 'prawn,'" he said, tapping out a
short percussive run, repeating it. "There's 'yawn,'" she said,
and put her hands down on his, holding the notes.

After Allen turned off the stove and poured off the boiling
water, they went upstairs, circling one under the other. He left
the light off, for the many-windowed room was full of light
from the one street lamp that had survived on the block. There
were shadows on the crazed plaster of the ceiling and the
bunched curtains nudged against the tall bed. They undressed

themselves and lay down on top of the coarse bedspread and
made love, Allen trying to disguise the earnestness of his
contraceptive measures. "Tomorrow is Father's Day," Gail
laughed. He did not think it was funny. Afterward they lay
talking with the little night breeze crossing them. They fell
asleep, cold on the damp spread, and a little later gathered
themselves under the sheet and cover and feel asleep again.

3

Gail was woken a little before dawn by the first twinges of
menstrual cramps. She slipped out of bed in the half light,
climbed downstairs for her handbag, then back upstairs to the
bathroom, shivering in the chill air. Afterwards she found
Allen's wretched-looking but snug flannel bathrobe in one of
the closets, slipped her sandals on, and went curving
downstairs once more. After rummaging about for the coffee
she found it finally in the refrigerator. She filled the pot and
set it over the fire. Only one burner on the old stove worked,
and that flamed up viciously at first and conceded to adjustment grudgingly.

While the coffee perked, Gail went into the living room and
curled up in a corner of the sofa, from where she could see out
into the front yard, just catching the first sun. "He makes his
scalloped way across the lawn," she said. Two priests wearing
identical homburgs were hurrying down Maiden Lane toward the cathedral, which was still almost invisible. It pleased
her, curled into the warm, rough corner of the sofa, the discomfort of her womb eased somewhat, the smell of coffee
drifting in, to see them about their peculiar business in the
early Sunday morning. She wondered if her kids were up yet,

and if they had remembered to get Steve something, and where he would take them.

She waited until the coffee had begun to boil over, and then a moment more, before getting up finally to turn it off. She poured two cups and climbed with care back up to the bedroom, where Allen lay curled tightly under the sheet, the spread bunched at the bed's foot. She sat carefully on her side of the bed, sipping from one cup, resting the other against her abdomen.

"Allen?" She spoke in a low voice, uncertain whether she wanted him to wake. He was sleeping with such intense concentration, his head driven into the pillow, his hair sticking out clownishly. "Allen?" He groaned, wrestled briefly, closely, with the pillow that was half-smothering him, then rolled over, his eyes suddenly wide open, confused. After a second he focused on her, smiled, and closed his eyes again. He settled back, his hand resting on the curve of her hip.

"Coffee?" she asked. He lay still for a moment, then sat up with a start that splashed coffee on her bare legs. He didn't even notice her yelp. "Jesus Christ, what time is it?" He tried to see the alarm clock on the dresser. "Christ, I'm supposed to be playing for early mass!" But he didn't get out of bed. He sat looking at Gail, who looked back at him with her eyebrows raised. He took the two coffee cups from her, set them on the window sill, then drew her down beside him, tangled in the long flannel robe.

"You'd better get going, pal," she said, and pushed him away lightly. He rose, unsure what she wanted him to do. After trying to get under the covers with her again he went and washed hastily and dressed. She frowned at his dark, unfashionable suit as she curled up under the cover, trying to organize the warmth of the clumsy robe. "You dress like a stiff," she said. He looked down at himself a moment, saw nothing wrong. "This is a clean shirt," he told her.

He drew the spread over her, kissed her, and was about to sit down on the bed, but she ordered him to leave. He hesitated, then pounded down the stairs. She could hear him gathering his music from the clutter on the piano downstairs, then heard the apartment and house doors slam. She rolled over and rested on one elbow, watching him run with his long, loose stride toward the cathedral, a bundle of music under his arm, his uncombed hair flying out crazily. "He looks ridiculous," she thought. She watched long after he was out of sight, then got up and went to his desk, sat down, and began searching for pencil and paper.

Father Olinsky was furious when Allen burst into the rear organ loft of the cathedral. The stocky, large-headed man glanced up only once, then bent again over the manuals, leading the first hymn. He was coatless, collarless. The black clerical shirt he wore was not fresh, and his wavy hair, usually so neatly plastered down, was almost as wild as Allen's. Olinsky lived in the residence next to the cathedral; the celebrant must have called him in a panic when Allen had not appeared. Only the large white button thanking you for not smoking was typical of the ordinarily impeccable priest's appearance. There was something odd about the organ, Allen thought.

When the hymn ended, Olinsky swung around on the bench and growled in a low voice, "Nice to see you, Heinz. Good of you to stop by." As director of music at the cathedral, Olinsky was Allen's immediate superior. They did not like each other.

"Sorry, Dick," Allen whispered as he slid into the spot Olinsky had just vacated. The bench was warm and a little moist there; Allen rested his weight on the front edge. As Allen arranged the music he would use as a postlude and checked the hymn list, Olinsky took a collar out of a pocket of the coat draped over a music stand. Grimacing, he fastened the collar, put on the coat, and smoothed down his hair. "O.K., Heinz," he said, in a gravelly voice that could barely be heard over the responses of the congregation. "I'm speaking to O'Donnel. This isn't the first time I've had to fill in for you." In a different, less querulous voice he added, "There's

something wrong with the damn organ. Needs overhauling,
don't you think?"

Allen was introducing the next hymn, one he had sung as a
child every mission Sunday in his father's church, anticipating
the noisy outdoor meal they would share with neighboring
congregations. He scarcely heard the deep, offended voice
promising to speak to him later. Allen was finally waking up
completely and was feeling good. His variations on the pedal
organ wandered away from the melody on the great —
Olinsky turned away in disgust.

The priest almost slammed the door of the loft as he stalked
out, but he caught himself and the heavy swinging door at the
last moment. The scattered voices of the congregation attend-
ing that early mass in no way interfered with Allen's en-
thusiastic, arhythmic, dissonant rendering of the beautiful old
hymn. Something was definitely funny, he decided; there was
a vague, wild undertone, like the wailing of a storm through a
ship's rigging. The chest is leaking, he thought. He liked the
effect and experimented with various stops to make the most
of it. Alone in the spacious loft, he sang along with great
feeling: "What though the spicy breezes Blow soft o'er
Ceylon's isle; Though ev'ry prospect pleases And only man is
vile; In vain with lavish kindness The gifts of God are strown;
The heathen in his blindness Bows down to wood and stone."

The casually dressed families, taking in an early mass so as
to get away early to lakes and golf courses, tried feebly to
assert themselves against the unnaturally raucous organ. As he
played, Allen could almost taste the summer Sundays with
long tables and folding wooden chairs on a church lawn, rows
of German Lutheran hot dishes and a wash bucket with a cake
of melting ice and cases of grape and orange Nehi and Dad's
Rootbeer. He plunged along with pleasure from verse to jin-
goistic verse. The people in the congregation glanced at each
other, puzzled, as stop after stop was added to Mason's old
hymn, crushing the enflamed and zealous text. From his high
seat near the altar the young priest who had been running

through the outline of his homily peered through the sunny, domed space up into the distant loft, but he could not see a thing.

For the 8:30 and 9:45 masses Allen played more sedately, and when Father Olinsky returned to take over for the later, better attended masses, returned in an improved mood and fresh clothes, Allen was unusually pleasant to him.

As he stepped out of one of the cathedral's side doors, Allen had to squint for a moment in the brilliant morning sun. He walked down Maiden Lane with his jacket slung over his shoulder, past the unused factory or warehouse of yellow brick, past the well-kept white house where the old man and woman were working in their neatly plowed little garden, past the branching dirt driveway under the dead catalpa trees of the big house with children.

He walked slowly, enjoying the sunshine, feeling hungry. From the vines overrunning the broken trellis behind a garage he pulled a handful of blue morning glories and noticed, as he straightened up again, a man dressed in a black suit, wearing white gloves, sunglasses, and a broad-brimmed black hat, carrying an open umbrella, disappear around the back of his house.

As he crossed the street, Allen looked up, shading his eyes, trying to see if Gail was at the window. But the windows returned only a gold glare from the midmorning sun. Something waved to him from high up on the roof, and his stomach tightened with a strange fear until he recalled the broken window and the dress he had stopped it up with. He took the porch steps three at a time, let himself in, singing at the top of his lungs in the cool passageway, "From Greenland's icy mountains . . . ." He went first into the kitchen, filled a glass of water for the already wilting flowers, then dashed up the winding stairs with them, water splashing out. "From many an ancient . . . ."

The bed was made, the room was somewhat straightened up, Gail was not there. He put the dripping glass with its

tangle of morning glories on some old exams on a corner of
the desk. The bathroom was empty. "Gail?" A space had been
cleared in the clutter of his desk. He leaned over and read the
note isolated in that little clearing. Her handwriting was small
and angular:

> He makes his scalloped way across the lawn;
> My love is sweet as lumber freshly sawn.
> His arching tail is ruffled by a breeze;
> My love is hidden as the hearts of trees.

4

"This will strike you as very funny, Heinz," growled the
burly priest. "You'll get a big kick out of this." Allen edged
through the litter of pipes and gathered workmen to where
one of the main organ chests, the one seemingly responsible
for most of the howling, had been drawn away from the rear
wall of the organ loft. He whistled. Dark water stains ran in a
slight diagonal down from the great round window, outlining
a jagged crack splitting down through the stone wall until it
disappeared into the floor. The varnished wood there was
water-warped and blistered, splitting away from the spreading stone. Allen put his fingertips into the crack, crouched,
and saw a glimmer of light slipping through the thick stone
blocks.

"Interesting?" asked the priest, his voice a barely controlled
snarl. "Amusing?" Allen felt for a moment that Olinsky held
him to blame. "That's what cracked the chest, I guess," he
said, straightening. "Water got in here and cracked it." "Brilliant," the priest snapped. "Sherlock Holmes. Now figure out
one more little detail, genius, and I'll shake your hand."

"What's that, Dick?" Allen asked, amused by the priest's ferocity. Olinsky thrust his thick head forward: "Why is the Cathedral of St. Paul splitting open like an overripe watermelon?" Allen thought it was a very worthwhile question, but he could not think of an answer. It's a sign, he said to himself. A sign of what?

Within the week a company of architectural engineers had been hired to assess the damage and undertake repairs on the cathedral. Allen had been spending a great deal of time in the loft among the dismantled pipes, helping the organ restorers sort and clean the corroded pipes, observing the carpentry work being done to the ruined chests. But when the engineers moved in to work on the wall, the portions of the organ that were still intact had to be shrouded and sealed in plastic and the rest moved to another building. As the chests were drawn farther from the wall, what had been the chaos of restoration became the orderliness of desperate measures. Holes were drilled into the stone piers, filling the blue- and red-stained air below the rose window with clouds of choking dust. After great bolts were driven into the holes, massive cables and massive turnbuckles were strung between the bolts and tightened slowly by sweating workmen.

Shortly after the architectural repairs began Allen brought Gail over to the cathedral to see what was going on. She was not terribly interested in either the disassembled organ or the splitting wall, for she had more immediate matters on her mind. Her husband had been exceptionally kind and reasonable recently — something she found disturbing. As a result she was in a fury to finish work on the children's rooms in Allen's house, even though they would not move in before the divorce was completed. Instead of looking at the damaged wall she kept staring out from the railing of the loft. "Never seen it from up here?" Allen asked. "I'd never been in the cathedral," she confessed. "I'm from Minneapolis, you know."

"Well!" he said. "Well well well. Come on downstairs

then, there's something you'll like." "I'd like to get back," she
protested, but he led her down the stairs from the loft,
through the nave, to the back of the towering brass grillwork
that separated the main altar from the crown of chapels that
formed a semicircle behind it. "Visit the Shrines of the Nations" a sign urged, pointing the way.

Each chapel focused on the heroic statue of a national saint,
backed up on either side by two subsidiary saints in stained
glass. After passing St. Anthony (Patron of the Italian People)
with Sanctus Franciscus and Sancta Clara, a very shaggy St.
John the Baptist (Patron of the French and Canadians) with
Sanctus Zacharius and Sanctus Simeon, and St. Patrick (Patron of the Irish People) with Sanctus Columbin and Sancta
Bridget, they came to a deep, oak-paneled doorway which led
to the angel-surmounted smaller building adjoining the rear
of the cathedral. In the entranceway to this door (which was
always locked) was a niche carpentered into the paneling,
with a little pan at the bottom. Above there was a chrome
faucet with a push button, as on a drinking fountain. A sign
above the faucet read:

> Holy
> Water
> For
> Home
> Use.

Allen showed her the sign and laughed with delight. Sometimes he walked around to the rear of the church solely to
look at the sign. Gail could not see the humor; the sign for
some reason annoyed her. Allen tried to explain the joke, but
it was difficult. "Don't you see? It's a washday miracle. Say
goodbye to . . . ," but she pulled him away and made him
shut up. He pushed the button before she got him away;
nothing happened. Nothing ever did.

They walked past the remaining Shrines of Nations in a
hurry: Saint Boniface, of the German People, with Sanctus
Bruno and Sancta Gertrude (stepping on a two-headed green

dragon); Saints Cyril and Methodius, of the Slavic Peoples, with Sanctus Stanislaus and Sanctus Wenceslaus; Saint Therese, "The Little Flower," Patroness of All Missions, with herself and Johannes. "Holy water," Gail said as they left the cool of the cathedral. "All water is holy."

Three summers of hard drought, separated by winters too cold for anything but a dusty powder snow that drifted restlessly from state to state across the Upper Midwest, had left the lawns of the city scorched brown and yellow. The little maples and ginkgoes that had been planted along the boulevards to replace the plague-stricken elms were blasted sticks. Iron posts would hold them upright until they rotted or were pulled up. The Mississippi was unnavigable far to the south; this far north it was a series of muddy pools and stagnant sloughs, stinking with the sewage that could no longer be washed away. The water table had dropped past all but the deepest wells, and the sandstone of the bluffs was turning brittle as the seemingly permanent moisture it held deep within it was gradually baked out. In several places houses perched on the bluffs had had to be abandoned when the shrinking stone of the bluffs split, crumbled, broke away beneath their foundations. No one could remember this happening before.

"It's probably an allergic reaction to the paint," he said. "Or else V.D." "Shut the hell up," she said, rubbing gingerly at the pimples and swollen area that had appeared on her wrists. "I'm sorry," he said, "it's probably not V.D." He stuck his brush into a can of thinner, wiped his hands on a rag, and looked more closely at the affected area. "Oh sister! Why don't you knock off for the day? Let's go for a walk. You need some fresh air, you're pale." Gail touched the swelling again. "We just started again, Allen," she complained. "We should be done with the whole wing by now, and we haven't even finished this one room. Don't you want us to be able to move in?"

Suddenly she was almost in tears, and Allen put his arm around her. "Of course I do. You know I do, I can't wait. Come on, what's the matter?" "I don't know," she answered. "I'm sorry, I just feel so bad." "Come on," he said, taking her brush from her, "you'll feel better after a nice walk." "We're never going to finish," she moaned, but allowed him to lead her toward the door.

As Gail and Allen were passing under the oak on the front lawn Annie called to them from the vacant lot where she and her brothers were working on their fort. "Hey, where do you think you're going?" Rick crawled out of the fort and Lewis seemed to be struggling with the canvas door on the inside. "Gail's not feeling well," Allen told them. "She's been breathing too much paint, so we're going for a little walk. We'll be back before it gets dark." "I think if Mom's sick we should stay with her," Rick said. "Yes," Annie agreed, "we'll go with you," and the three children ran across the lot to join them. "O.K.," Allen said, "but take it easy."

Lewis took his mother's hand and the five of them walked down Maiden Lane toward the cathedral. As they passed the yellow brick building at the crook in the lane Annie went over to investigate a sign posted on the door. "What does this mean, 'adjoining property?'" she asked. Allen said, "Read what the rest of it says." She read in a formal tone, emphasizing with her voice what was typographically emphasized on the sign. "Notice!" she began, "Entry To This Building *Is Forbidden*. This Building Is *DANGEROUS* To Life, Limb, and Adjoining Property." In a whisper she added, "by order of St. Paul Police Department." "It means," Allen told her, "that the place is ready to collapse and when it does it'll demolish the neighborhood. Adjoining property is the neighborhood. 'There goes the neighborhood,' we'll say. Better stay away from there, Annie." "Oh Allen, you're crazy. That's not right, is it Mom?" "It's sort of right," she answered. "Let's keep moving; I'm getting the shivers standing here."

When they reached the cathedral Allen tried a number of doors, in the hope of letting the kids see how everything was coming apart. But the doors were locked and he had no key. Instead he led them around to the front and showed them the scaffolding towering up to the dark rose window and the drilling equipment that was being used to take core samples from the ground around the foundations. Gail started to shiver again and they were about to go back when Annie shot off down the long, steep series of steps leading down the side of the bluff. Rick followed her, and Lewis, torn for a moment between security and adventure, opted for adventure by breaking away from Gail and struggling down the stone steps. All three ignored Allen's orders to come back; in a minute Annie, then Rick, disappeared behind the end of the cast-iron fence that protected the steps from a gully cutting back into the bluff.

"I'll never make it up those stairs again, Allen," Gail said. "Will you go get them?" She was hugging herself and shuddered. The swelling on her wrists had gotten worse and the pimples were starting to turn dark and pustular in the center. He looked at her. "I think we should get you to a doctor." "It can wait. Just get the kids and we can go back." She sat down on the top step while Allen ran after the children. He passed Lewis near the bottom and told him to start back up, then found the place where the other two had disappeared.

The gully was deeper than he had thought, slicing far into the slope of the bluff, filled with the dried stalks of weeds. Rusty tracks ran out of the ravine, stopping at the street that circled the bluff. "Oh great," he said to himself. At the deep end of the gully Rick and Annie were talking to an old man with a beard — the same man, Allen later realized, who hauled junk on a bicycle. They were standing before what seemed to be the mouth of a tunnel, covered with wire mesh that was twisted and buckled where the lip of the tunnel had caved in. Debris of sandstone littered the entrance.

"Come on!" he shouted at them. "We have to get back." They hesitated a moment, gave a last look into the opening in the bluff, then ran to meet him. He tried to hurry them a little, but the steps were very steep. Finding Lewis about where he had passed him he lifted him onto his shoulders and trudged up the steps with Annie behind him and Rick in front. "That man was real nice, Allen," Annie said. "How nice?" Allen was starting to breathe with difficulty — Lewis was heavier than he had thought. "He told us that that was an old trolley tunnel," Annie said, "which is sort of a train, he said, and it used to go almost under the cathedral and under where your place is and came up onto Selby and went across the Lake Street bridge into Minneapolis. I think that would be great, going under your house in a train. I was in one once, with Rick and Mom and Dad, but not Lewis, he wasn't born yet." "I *was* born!" Lewis shrieked over Allen's head. "I *was!*" "Don't you think that would be great, Allen?" Annie continued. "The man said you couldn't go into the tunnel now because it was starting to fall in, but they hadn't used it in a long time anyway." Allen grunted; he was worried about Gail, and his legs were starting to go mushy from the long climb. He wished to God that the kids were not there; it seemed like too much. "How would you like to walk for a while, Lewis?" "No sir!" Lewis answered, "This is fine."

At the top of the steps Allen put the protesting Lewis down and helped Gail to her feet. She was sweating and shivering; the children grew quiet when they saw her. When they got back to the house it was nearly dark. Allen switched on the lights, got a blanket to wrap around Gail's shoulders, then hunted for and finally found his car keys. "You kids be good," Allen said. "We're going to the doctor to find out what's the matter with Gail. It might be late before we get back. Annie, you're in charge; you all can sleep in the bed upstairs when you get sleepy." "We should go along with you," she said. Allen didn't think so. Lewis started crying. When Allen helped Gail out the door, Rick and Annie were trying to comfort him, proposing various diversions.

The big county hospital was only about a mile from Allen's place. He took the shortest route he knew, but soon came to a detour where part of the dry sandstone cliffs had collapsed onto the pavement. The alternate route took him farther to the south than he had intended and he was stopped again, this time by the new interstate that was being cut through town. There was no apparent way to get around it, though he could almost see the lights of the hospital's top floors. "Allen, where are you going?" Gail moaned, shivering under the blanket. Noting that her swollen wrists were oozing a dark pus, she tried to hold them so they would not stain the blanket, though it was old and worn. "You just take it easy," he said. "Just lean back and relax. We'll be there in a minute. Goddamn freeway had me confused, but we're almost there." He was in a part of town which seemed totally unfamiliar. Old buildings were being torn down, there seemed to be no street signs, and the streets were deserted. "We're almost there," he said, feeling the cold sweat run down his sides.

Allen drove down one street after another, losing all sense of direction. Then, as he passed the wreckage of a large brick building with demolition equipment looming up in the darkness, he noticed some people next to a parked car. He spun the old Volvo into a U-turn that slammed Gail against the door. Too relieved to think of apologizing, he pulled up beside the car and asked the people if they knew how to get to the county hospital from there. There might have been a closer hospital, but he was incapable of introducing another unknown into the situation. He would have driven fifty miles to get to a hospital that he knew.

"Well, you are surely in luck," the woman beside the car told him. She spoke with a soft Tennessee accent and was holding an armload of old bricks. "That fellow there," she gestured toward the grizzled man being helped into the car, "has taken a nasty cut on his hand, and my husband and I are taking him in to get patched up. You just follow along." Before she got into the driver's seat the woman dumped the armload of bricks into the back of the battered Volkswagen squareback, which groaned on its springs. Her husband was in the back seat wrapping a handkerchief around the hand of the injured man, who chuckled softly, his head lolling slightly on his shoulders. Allen followed the heavily loaded Volkswagen and arrived at the hospital within a few minutes.

Of the emergency room Allen remembered very little afterwards. Since things were slow, it being a Sunday night, Gail was almost at once led away from him. The staff greeted by name the wine-reeking derelict who had been brought in by the southern woman and her husband. "What did you do this time, Freddy?" an orderly asked, unwrapping the handkerchief. The man just gave a low, throaty chuckle, letting his head roll back against the wall. "Wheeee boy!" he exclaimed, grinning, "wheeeee boy!" passively holding out his bleeding hand.

Allen spent some time filling in admittance and insurance forms for Gail, guessing about dates and other information. Then he sat down in the waiting room beside an old man with bandaged arm who was berating himself in an angry, disgusted voice. "What a stupid thing to do," the old man said again and again. Finally the old woman who had come in with him snapped, "Hush now, you expected a smart accident? All accidents are stupid. Now hush."

After an hour or so a doctor came out, drew Allen aside, and told him that Gail was suffering from cutaneous anthrax. "Anthrax is hardly ever fatal in this form," she said, "except when it gets into the blood. We seem to have caught it in time, though I wish she had been brought in sooner. She's getting antibiotics now; we'll keep her here for a few days at least." "Can I see her?" "Not tonight," the doctor said, "she's been given a sedative. Are you the husband?" "The husband? No, not the husband. The friend." "I see," she said in a flat voice. "Well, you might see that some of her personal things are brought over tomorrow." "Yes, I'll see to that. I didn't think people got anthrax anymore." "She says she works in a yarn shop. They've probably gotten in some imported fibers that hadn't been sterilized. The other people who work there should come in to be inoculated, and the place will have to be closed until we run it down."

Allen gave her the name of the woman who owned the shop, asked again to be allowed to see Gail, and was again refused. He drove home, parked beneath the oak tree, and crept carefully into the house. The lights were all on and the baby grand piano was shrouded to the floor with blankets and towels and the bathroom rug, all held in place with books stacked on the lid.

As he stood before it, his mind a blank, Annie cautiously crawled out from between two hanging blankets. "Hi Allen," she whispered. "Lewis was afraid, so we made a fort to sleep in. How's Mom?" Allen sat down on the floor beside her. "She's pretty sick, but they say she'll be all right. They want to keep her in the hospital for a few days to be sure." "O.K.," Annie said. "Maybe we can visit her tomorrow. You look awful." "I'm just tired. How about you, haven't you been asleep?" "I was," she said, "but I woke up when you came in. I'm a light sleeper when I'm in charge of the kids." "That's good," Allen said. "But now you'd better get back to sleep."

"Would you like to join us in our fort?" Annie asked. Allen lifted up a corner, peered in under the piano. Rick and Lewis were sprawled under a tangle of blankets. "I think it would be a little crowded," he said. "I think I'll lie down here, outside your door. How's that?" "That would be very nice, Allen," Annie replied, starting to crawl back under the piano. "Now I can really sleep." Allen got up and turned out most of the lights in the room, leaving one lamp on low. Then he lay down on his back and stretched out, one hand resting lightly on the bottom folds of the wall of the children's fort. When he finally fell asleep he drove again and again down the endless lost road toward the hospital. Not once, all night, did he reach it in time.

6

Allen had determined to finish at least one room of the east wing of the house while Gail was recuperating. There was not too much to do anymore, though it would be time-consuming: he had to paint trim, clean up baseboards, and replace fixtures. But when he stepped outside, the early morning was as inviting as fresh sheets. The sun filtering under the dark of oak leaves caught the bright edge of the pointing tool he had left lying on the porch. He picked up the tool, rubbed off the few new specks of dew rust with a handful of brick dust, and gave the wall a few trial digs. He was not so good at patching in the new mortar, which was always too thick or thin to work in properly, and already the front wall was gouged into deep relief. He worried about the wall collapsing, but still probed and dug between the soft bricks.

He turned suddenly, feeling himself watched, but the street was empty. The field beside his lot concealed rabbits in the wiry wild grass, but the old man who had stopped for a moment on his heavy bicycle to readjust the load of rusty angle iron had already coasted past the dogleg of Maiden Lane, and so was out of sight. Remembering with displeasure that he had to be at the university early that afternoon to give organ lessons, Allen bent back to the soothing, rhythmic work.

By ten the sun was lost in the oak. Allen would have to start mortaring or the whole east wall would sag down upon itself. The gray and rotten boards of the porch glistened under the hose flood as he struggled to get the consistency right, adding water and cement by turns, stirring with an old piece of lathe, until he had mixed far more than he would be able to use up that morning.

A car honked nasally as he was easing the first trowel-load between the bricks. He started, flipping mortar onto a window, and turned in annoyance. Then he saw that it was Elizabeth's red Fiat, and it was Elizabeth getting out. His chest went tight. "Hi Allen," she called. Elizabeth, who had married him one time and left another time. He stood with his hands thick with mortar as she came up onto the porch and gave him a small, cool kiss.

"Wait here," he said, wiping his hands on his trousers. He went inside and returned with two kitchen chairs and a jug of iced tea that sloshed over onto the porch. He didn't want her inside, although he could not have said why. He went back in for a couple of glasses, and she followed him, ignoring his instructions to make herself comfortable on the porch. As Allen washed two glasses in the overcrowded sink Elizabeth wandered around in the living room of the house she had left almost a year before. It was not much changed, except for the piano.

She laughed, "What's this all about, Allen?" "Oh, that. That's a fort. Gail's kids made it while I was taking her to the hospital. I haven't had time to clear it off." "I heard about that," she said. "Anthrax — strange. How is she?" "She's been home for a few days now. There was some blood poisoning, it seems, but they caught it in time. She'll be all right." "Well," she said. "Well?" They went back out to the porch and Allen poured two glasses of cloudy tea. They sat beside each other on the littered porch, looking out toward the cathedral.

"Well," she said, "what've you been doing? Are you teaching summer school?" "No summer school," he said, wincing at the bitter tea. "Give lessons two afternoons a week, work on the house. Work on the house a lot. Sit on the porch a lot." He hurled the contents of his glass over the railing.

"You always liked the house, didn't you," Elizabeth remarked. Allen began fiddling with the pointing tool and now reached back awkwardly, jabbing at a brick's rotten edge. "I guess," he said. "You sure you don't want it?" She shook her head. "It's a mill stone, Allen. I'm a musician, not a contractor. And I don't need the money, let's not start on that." "Great," he said. "It's a divorce made in heaven." She didn't laugh, only sipped at her tea in silence, thinking that she had laughed too many times.

"I think I have the job with Seattle," she said. "You think?" "Well, I have it. It isn't supposed to get around until they make it official." "That's great!" he exclaimed, feeling a genuine pleasure that was in no way diminished by the pure and burning jealousy that he simultaneously experienced. "This calls for a celebration." He rose, took her glass and poured it over the railing, then went back into the house. "Allen?" she called in to him. "Allen, I have to be at the Hall in a little while. We have to talk. Seriously." He returned with two bottles of beer and handed her one. "Here's to Seattle!" "Allen, it's ten A.M." "That late?" he said, taking a long pull from the foaming bottle. "I was going to finish painting the front bedroom this morning. Well, a celebration's a celebration."

She put her bottle down on the porch. "We have to talk," she said. "I'll be leaving in a month or so and we should settle as much as possible before then." "Settle? What's to settle?" "You do want to go through with this, don't you?" He finished the beer. "How could you doubt me? You sure you don't want this?" He reached for the bottle she had put down. "What are you going to do, Allen?" "I'm going to drink your beer."

Her mouth tightened and she sat up straighter. "Is Gail

going to move in?" Allen drank long and deeply, rested the bottle on his knee, and belched. "Funny you should ask. It seems Steve, that's her almost-ex, moved back in to take care of the kids while she was in the hospital, and he's still there, cooking and doing the housework. They seem to be getting along real well. So who the hell knows what's going to happen." The bottle tipped off his knee and crashed to the porch floor. He rose and opened the screen door. "Get you another while I'm up?" He waited, shrugged, went in.

When he returned, carrying two opened bottles, Elizabeth was standing on the walk before the porch, leaning uneasily against one of the stone pillars. "Allen," she said, looking down, "maybe we should put this off for a while. You could come out to Seattle, we could try it again." Allen stared at her, his hands clutching the two bottles by their necks. "How about what's-his-name?" "I don't love what's-his-name," she answered. "That's all over. I just needed some distance for a while, I felt like I couldn't rely on you. Now I don't think I need what I needed then." "Well," he said. "Well well well." He sat down clumsily on one of the chairs, still clutching the bottles. "And what'd I do in Seattle?" "You'd have work," she said, "you're good. You'd have time to compose if you got away from this goddamn house." He drank abstractedly from one bottle, then from the other. "Well well well," he said. After another minute Elizabeth turned without a word and walked to her car and drove away. "Well well well," Allen said, drinking deeply. "Well well well well." He drank again. "What does she mean, she couldn't rely on me?" he asked. "What the hell does she want? What the blue hell does anyone want?"

When Elizabeth had gone, Allen came down from the porch and dropped into his familiar spot underneath the oak, twin spouts shooting up from the bottles as he landed with a grunt. "Well I guess," he said. He stayed there for a long time, then remembered the lessons he had to give that afternoon. He went in, cleaned up, then drove unsteadily to the university. A pall of acrid smoke, now almost permanent, hung over the freeway from grass fires burning a few miles from the city. Heat shimmered up from the roadway and fire sirens wailed in the distance.

The lessons themselves, given in the university chapel, seemed to go on forever. Allen stood behind the sweating students as they tried to coordinate their hands and feet in some semblance of rhythm and accuracy. One student, who showed promise, bobbed and nodded over the keyboard until Allen grabbed the long, curling hair at the nape of his neck and forced him to be still while he was playing. Some of the students were offended when they smelled the alcohol on Allen's breath, others smiled secret smiles. Throughout the afternoon Allen said very little, making only the most perfunctory remarks. He stood behind the students, his legs feeling rubbery, scarcely noticing the awkwardness and occasional success.

The lessons finally over, Allen locked the organ, found his car in the huge university lot, and started driving home. He decided to stop over at Gail's house, but got lost in the detours necessitated by the freeway construction. "I've been here before," he muttered. "Is this a sign?" It was a question he had taken to asking himself the last few weeks. "Is this a sign?" He had no idea what he meant.

At last he found the development where Gail lived, and after driving around the curving streets of identical houses he found her place. Steve was there. He greeted Allen shyly. "Taking my vacation," he confessed. After directing Allen solicitously to Gail's room he went outside with Lewis. Lewis grinned up at Allen as if it were a marvelous joke. It occurred to Allen that it might be.

Gail was in bed. She looked tired, almost limp, but her face colored when Allen entered her room. After talking for a while about how she felt and how things were at the shop he said to her abruptly, "You're going to stay with him, aren't you," despising himself for the small surge of relief he sensed in the midst of a great flood of loss. Gail's fist clenched and unclenched on the cover. "He's just been very nice, Allen. I can't help it. It's like it was before the kids." It was not anthrax that dug into her face. Allen sat on the corner of the bed, then stood up. "What are you going to do?" he asked. "What do you want me to do?" He was quiet a long time, and she barely heard him when he answered, "I don't know." She looked away. "Then we'll just have to see." He considered telling her about Elizabeth's visit, but the thought of talking through that, of talking anymore about anything, was more than he could stand. She's so far away, he thought. Everyone is so far away — how can anyone talk? Stopping for a red light on the way home he thought, she's in good hands, and then stared at himself in the maladjusted rearview mirror until an angry blare of horns finally jarred him into motion again.

7

"What the hell?" Allen shouted. "What the goddamn hell?" He stood at the curb before his house, shaking in rage and disbelief. A mountain of green rose up before him, a heaped sea of dark green leaves towering up from his lawn, spilling over the curb into a detritus of broken twigs and torn clusters of leaves. He roared then at the bare-chested, bronze young man working on the massive lower limbs, but no one heard him above the shrieking of the chain saw. Allen grabbed a dead, broken limb from the street and ran at the man, who shouted with surprise when the branch crashed into the saw, splintered, set the hooped chain of teeth bouncing to one side, jamming into the ground, dying into sudden silence.

The boy backed off and two other workers came running

from the green truck that was parked down the street. One of them, a fat, middle-aged man in a baseball cap, grabbed the stub of the branch away from Allen and pushed him back from the glowering boy with the dead saw. The air reeked with the smell of gasoline and the wet pungent odor of fresh-cut oak.

"What's going on here, now?" the fat man asked in a voice at once soothing and wary. "You acting crazy, pal — what's the trouble?" Allen stared down at the broad, glistening stump cut into crazy planes, a tall splintered ridge running through the center. The huge trunk, sawn into sections, lay as it had fallen. The fat man's shirt hung open on either side of his big brown belly. "Did," Allen finally managed to get out, choking on the words he was trying to say. "Why you . . . ." The fat man looked at him with shrewd, pale eyes.

"You live here, pal?" the man asked. Allen nodded dully. "Well now, listen. We been cutting trees around here for years. This one ain't special. Because it's yours, that don't make it special." Allen choked, then exploded, "This is an *oak!* " and lunged at the grinning boy with the chain saw. The fat man grabbed Allen with astonishing quickness, whirled him around without stopping his motion, and pushed, pressed him effortlessly down onto the fresh, wet stump, jammed him down easily, dropping him where the ridge of splinters would not spear him. Allen sat, surprised, palms pressed down against the wet wood, staring up at the fat man who had put him there. The boy with the saw stepped around from behind the fat man who stood over Allen impassively. "There's such a thing as oak wilt," the boy said triumphantly.

Allen started to jump up again, but again the fat man had pushed him back down before he knew what had happened. Allen stared at the chewed, chip-littered ground between his feet. "Show me a sign of it," he said. "Show me one wilt-ed . . . ." The fat man interrupted him, his face expressionless. "It's down," he said. "Get used to it. It was marked and we cut it down. That's our job. Whether it was sound or sick don't make a bit of difference anymore. So get used to it." He stood looking down at Allen for a minute, then walked toward the green truck, gesturing to the other two men to take up their equipment and follow him. "It's late, boys," Allen heard him say. "We'll finish in the morning."

For a long time after the truck had driven away Allen sat on the stump, cold moisture soaking up through his trousers. A yard up from him on the huge horizontal trunk he could see the ring of red paint that had been the sign of ruin. After a while he got up and went into the house. He went into the kitchen and found he had finished the last of his beers that morning. After hunting around he discovered an unopened bottle of expensive scotch which Elizabeth and he had received for Christmas several years before. He sat at the table and started to drink and didn't stop until his head sagged down onto his arms on the table.

He woke a few hours later. It had grown dark; he found himself hunched over the table in the dark hot kitchen, a half bottle of scotch beside him. He felt awful and poured himself another drink, and then one more. He stood up then, knocking his chair onto the floor. "Beddy," he said. "Time for teddy beddy." He laughed a harsh, animal laugh that turned into a giggle at the end, then began feeling his way to the front of the house.

The living room was white with moonlight flooding through the tall circle of windows. He had never seen it so full of light, even in the brilliant, brittle nights of high winter. Allen stood unsteadily grasping the smooth, upward curving railing of the spiral staircase that led up to his bedroom. "Teddy beddy," he said, looking up. Then he shook his head. "Hair flies sadness." He let himself slip to the bare wooden floor, sat there for a time, then crawled to the blanket-shrouded piano. He gave a low laugh. "Sleepy ina fort," he announced, and crawled through the blankets into the darkness under the piano, where he curled up and fell into a dreamless sleep.

8

These are the facts. The collapse of the Summit Hill bluff in the region of the cathedral began sometime between 5:30 and 6:00 A.M. It seems to have been triggered by the caving in of the old Selby Avenue trolley tunnel, which is reported to have been deteriorating for a number of weeks. Possibly the tunnel merely gave direction to a collapse that was caused by some other weakness. In any case, the main destruction ran along the course of the tunnel from below the cathedral to near the corner of Selby and Farrington. Houses thirty to a hundred yards on either side of this line were damaged or destroyed. Surprisingly, only two lives were lost — an elderly man and woman who were crushed to death in bed in their home on Maiden Lane.

The most spectacular destruction, of course, was the collapse of the cathedral itself. The great weight of the cathedral on the edge of the bluff probably contributed to the sudden and massive crumbling of the hill that overlooked downtown St. Paul. Once the cave-in began, the cathedral seems to have tilted and collapsed, sliding forward with a portion of the brittle sandstone bluff on which it was built. It now lies in a mountain of gray stone and rubble. "An elephant sliding down a haystack" was the way one observer described the event.

Allen woke with a tremendous hangover and the smell of plaster dust in his nose. Sneezing, he stared up at the underside of the piano, than pushed out against one of the blanket walls. Nothing happened. Then he noticed that the rugs and covers on all sides bulged in at odd angles and in fact left him only a little room. He lay back again, closed his eyes for a few moments, then looked up and around again. The air was still thick with dust and sirens screamed somewhere in the neighborhood. He pushed out at what he discovered to be the brick and lathe and plaster ruins of his house until he found a side, where the windows had been, that yielded slightly.

Gradually, his head throbbing and his stomach turning over, he dug his way toward the surface, saw light, and finally pushed himself into the open. As he stood up, staggering down from the wreckage, a cop ran by across the crazy, heaped ground. "Hey!" he shouted, "you O.K.? Anyone else in there?" Allen assured him that he was fine, although he felt anything but, and that no one else was trapped in the house. When the cop ran off, Allen stumbled around in his yard, then looked toward the dusty gap of sky where the cathedral had once loomed. The only building still standing along the line to the ex-cathedral was the old yellow brick building at the bend of Maiden Lane.

Without understanding why, Allen gazed for a long time toward the building, feeling that something still was uncompleted. After a while he realized that what he was waiting for was the old man on the lady's bicycle. He felt certain, somehow, that the old man would appear, would ride by to tell him it was over, to tell him what it meant. But the old man did not appear, though Allen stared steadily eastward until he was almost blinded by the newly risen sun burning orange and yellow through the smoke above the city.